Enforcer Knossis Raund doesn't know why Fate has forsaken him. He meets his mate, only to discover she's a happily married woman in a great marriage with several kids. Refusing to bring heartbreak to the family, Knossis seeks out the one thing he can think of that will allow him to still have a sex life—a vampire's bite.

As a vampire wrangler, Chissom Minscote is confident in his abilities. He knows Knossis expects to be bitten by a female vampire. Except, none are available, and the handsome shifter is desperate to feel . . . something. Chissom is happy to help.

Hank Everly is a human who's been working as a donor for over ten years. He loves the thrill of the bite, but he knows never to get attached. When Chissom asks Hank to help him show a lonely and heartbroken shifter a relaxing evening, he's happy to help the handsome pair.

An unexpected attack, a myriad of injuries, and the intervention of a Horseman of the Apocalypse bring the trio to a crossroads—accept the bond of Famine so they can bring their attackers to justice or die. Can the group learn to care for and trust each other as they unweave the twisting plot against them?

Famine's Foursome
Copyright © 2021 Charlie Richards
ISBN: 978-1-4874-3339-0
Cover art by Angela Waters

Published by eXtasy Books Inc or
Devine Destinies, an imprint of eXtasy Books Inc

Look for us online at:
www.eXtasybooks.com or www.devinedestinies.com

Famine's Foursome
A Loving Nip Book Twenty-Five

By

Charlie Richards

DEDICATION

Keep trying. Stay humble. Trust your instincts. Most importantly,
act. When you come to a fork in the road, take it.
~Yogi Berra

CHAPTER ONE

Enforcer Knossis Raund stared at the picture, sadness twisting his gut. Bowing his head, he closed his eyes for a few seconds, just breathing. Knossis lifted his head and focused once more on the photo.

Lifting a trembling hand, Knossis tapped his phone, bringing up a row of icons at the top. He hit the garbage can, deleting the picture. Then he exited the gallery and cleared his trash for good measure.

Knossis tossed his phone onto his desk, then leaned back in his chair. He sighed deeply, resting his head against the back. As he stared at the ceiling, he sent soothing thoughts to the whining fox in his mind.

"Hey, Knoss. You okay?"

Turning his head, Knossis eyed Bristol Luderm, their fox skulk's new beta. After Cain had denied Alpha Ferris's order—Ferris also happened to be Cain's father—to wed a woman instead of bonding with his mate, the nearby vampire coven had helped Cain report Ferris's actions to the Shifter Council. The council had sent an investigator, who'd decided Ferris was abusing his authority, and he'd been removed as alpha.

Their skulk had rallied around their beta, Wilfred, and had accepted him as alpha. That had left the beta position open because Knossis had declined it. He preferred being the head enforcer and didn't want the responsibility of leading.

"Knoss?"

Blinking, Knossis forced himself to answer truthfully, since

1

their new beta would be able to scent a lie, anyway. "I met my mate." Upon seeing Bristol begin to grin, Knossis grimaced and shook his head. "I can't have her. She's already taken."

Bristol's eyes widened, and his lips parted, betraying his shock as much as his scent did. Striding into the room, he went straight to the bar. He glanced Knossis's way as he grabbed the whiskey decanter and two crystal tumblers. Then Bristol settled in a cushioned chair in the lounge area of the office.

"Sit," Bristol ordered, using the tip of the decanter to point at a chair next to his own. "Now."

Knossis pushed from his seat and obeyed, moving around the room. Unable to help himself, he flopped onto the chair Bristol had indicated while heaving a big sigh. When Bristol handed him a tumbler of whiskey, he knocked it back in one go.

Bristol immediately leaned forward and refilled it.

Sighing again, Knossis rested the tumbler against his temple and closed his eyes.

"So, talk to me, Knoss," Bristol urged. "Where and when did you meet her, and what kind of relationship is she in?"

Cracking his eyelids back open, Knossis told his beta, "I met her in passing three months ago."

Bristol's brows lifted a smidge, and his lips tightened. "And?"

Knossis leaned forward. Resting his forearms on his thighs, he cradled his tumbler between his palms. He licked his lips before starting from the beginning.

"I went to Barney's to rent a horse and take a trail ride," Knossis explained slowly, referring to a skulk-owned barn that leased horses and offered lessons. "A woman was there watching her daughter, who was taking a lesson. I realized she was my mate as soon as I walked into the barn." Smiling sadly, Knossis whispered, "Her divine scent stood out over all the smells of horse, shavings, manure, and leather."

"I've been told that a mate's scent is beyond anything we've ever enjoyed before," Bristol whispered, his tone encouraging. "I'm assuming it's not due to her having a kid that's stopping you."

Waving to his huge frame — Knossis knew his massive, six-foot-four body could be intimidating — he explained, "I said hello, and she was afraid of me. I could smell it." His mass was a good thing for an enforcer, but it made approaching a diminutive, five-foot-four-inch woman tough. "I smiled, was friendly, asked about her kid, talked about the riding facility and how Barney is a friend. Stuff like that." Recalling the memory, Knossis had to smile. He'd been so damn excited. "She was just beginning to relax when her husband arrived to pick up her and their daughter."

"Ouch," Bristol muttered, wincing in sympathy.

Knossis nodded before taking a sip of his whiskey. "You know how people say that Fate brings mates together when they need each other?"

Bristol grunted, tipping his chin. "I've heard that."

Clearing his throat, Knossis admitted, "At first, I thought Fate was bringing me into her life to save her from an abusive husband." He met Bristol's gaze. "That's not the case."

Frowning, Bristol picked up the decanter and refilled Knossis's glass.

Knossis wasn't even certain when he'd drained it, and he accepted the liquor gratefully. "I discreetly asked Barney for their information, so I could look into them." After taking another sip, Knossis admitted, "Then I spied on them whenever I safely could." Sadness flooded him as he recalled the things he'd seen. His voice came out strained as he admitted, "He's a great husband, a stable provider, and a fantastic father." Knossis met Bristol's gaze and stated, "I have no idea why Fate would show me a mate that it would be wrong to try to

3

claim. I can't break up that happy family just because Fate decided she's mine. It would be wrong."

Bristol stayed quiet for several long minutes, staring into his own tumbler of whiskey. Finally lifting his gaze, he murmured, "And you're certain they're a good match?"

Blushing, Knossis nodded. "They live on a small farm." Grimacing, he added, "I could get pretty damn close . . . including looking in their bedroom window."

Wincing, Bristol whispered, "I bet watching any activity in the bedroom required a hell of a lot of self-control."

Knossis blew out a harsh breath. "I just about leaped through the window," he admitted, rubbing the back of his neck. "That was when I realized I had to stop visiting for a while and think."

"And how long ago was that again?" Bristol asked softly, frowning.

"I met her three months ago," Knossis admitted. "I didn't say anything to anyone because our skulk was in such a state of flux. I—" He cut himself off, uncertain what else to say.

Bristol rubbed a palm over his face. "That explains why you've been so quiet ever since I arrived." His expression turned wry. "I just thought you were wary of the new guy."

Lifting his brows, Knossis quickly shook his head. "No, Beta."

Scoffing, Bristol rolled his eyes. "Relax, Knoss," he rumbled, a pained look creasing his features. "I'm just explaining. It also explains why some of the people in our skulk have given you worried looks." Bristol smiled sadly as he admitted, "I know you said you didn't want the beta position, but I've still been a bit worried you were going to create trouble."

Knossis frowned into his drink for a few seconds before focusing on Bristol. "I'm sorry. I thought I was handling it better."

Nodding, Bristol told him, "It's good that you've shared

your problem. Now we can help you." Then his brows furrowed. "Are you absolutely certain you don't want to pursue your mate?"

Shaking his head, Knossis whispered, "She's happy where she is." He returned his focus to Bristol. "I can't ruin that."

Reaching over, Bristol squeezed Knossis's knee briefly. "You're a good man, Knoss." He swigged back his whiskey before picking up the decanter again. After refilling his glass, he offered to do the same to Knossis's, which he happily accepted. Once they were relaxed in their chairs again, Bristol asked, "So, you're not going after her. I get that. What are you going to do?"

Knossis hadn't wanted to think that far ahead, but he knew he needed to. Furrowing his brows, he stared at the amber liquid in his glass as he swirled it around the container. He didn't know how to answer Bristol's question.

"What I mean is," Bristol continued, leaning toward him. "We can help you keep your fox in check when we go out running, the alpha and I." Cocking his head, he gave him a searching look. "Which leaves a shifter's high sex drive. Can you handle celibacy?"

Opening his mouth, Knossis froze. Then he snapped his jaw shut again. He grimaced as he tightened his hold on his glass. A second later, Knossis took a quick swig of his whiskey, hoping the mild burn of the high-end liquid would help clear his head.

Bristol cleared his throat, redrawing Knossis's attention. "You're going to need a work-around while you and your animal come to grips with allowing your mate to pass you by for the next few decades." Offering a small smile, he added, "And we'll find a way to discreetly encourage them to move out of state" —lifting his hands, Bristol added—"to their benefit, don't worry. That way, it'll be easier for your animal to pine and move on."

5

Knossis sighed deeply, nodding as he processed Bristol's words. His beta had a point. There was no way he could remain celibate for the next thirty-plus years or however long it took his mate to grow old and die.

Just thinking about the beautiful woman who he and his fox were enamored with dying, Knossis felt his gut clench. Still, he knew that due to his decision to walk away from her, it was exactly what would happen. She was a human. She would grow old and die long before Knossis would.

Appreciating the support, and the outside opinion, Knossis focused on Bristol and asked, "What do you suggest?"

Bristol narrowed his eyes and smiled. "Our skulk is on good terms with the nearby vampire coven now that Ferris has been removed from power, right?"

Knossis nodded once, not understanding where Bristol was going.

His beta shrugged and offered a roguish smile. "While I've never experienced it myself, I hear that a vampire bite can be orgasmic. Maybe you should consider it."

Two months later, Knossis did just that, seeking out an audience with Master Dante Mannis.

CHAPTER TWO

Chissom Minscote couldn't remember the last time he'd been called into Master Dante's office. Since he knew he hadn't done anything wrong, he was more curious than nervous. Pausing at the door, he knocked and waited.

"Come in, Chissom."

Obeying Dante's order, Chissom entered and glanced around the room. His master was alone, sitting behind his desk. He pushed his laptop off to the side and leaned his forearms on the desk.

"I've had a request from a shifter," Dante told him without preamble as Chissom eased into a chair across from him. "Feel free to refuse."

Tipping his head in interest, Chissom waited for his master to explain.

Dante folded his hands before him and asked him, "Have you bitten a shifter before?"

Chissom straightened, surprised at the question. "I have." Something clicked, and he jumped to a conclusion. "Is there a shifter here asking for a vampire bite?"

"There is," Dante confirmed.

Grinning, anticipation filling him, Chissom looked forward to sampling whoever it was. He hadn't seduced a shifter in almost eighty years. Vampires and shifters didn't exactly run in the same circles.

"He asked for a female vampire," Dante told him. "But Marian doesn't like shifter blood, Lidia is out working, Sandra is in town, and the others are bonded."

7

"And this shifter is in a hurry?" Chissom asked, rubbing the back of his neck. "Been a while since I seduced a supposed straight guy."

Dante winced. "He's a bit desperate. Yes." After a second, he shared, "He met his mate and can't have her, so he's struggling with, well, sex."

"Aaaah," Chissom murmured, figuring there had to be far more to the story. "And he's come to us for help."

"Exactly," Dante confirmed. "Do you want to try to give him a . . . hand?"

Chissom snorted softly. "Sure."

"He's in the green room."

Rising to his feet, Chissom felt honored his master had such faith in him. "I'll do what I can to help."

Dante nodded and eased back in his seat. "Good luck."

Rising to his feet, Chissom began toward the door. "Thank you."

When Chissom reached the door, Dante called, "Oh, his name is Knossis. He's an enforcer for the nearby fox shifter skulk."

Chissom paused with his hand on the knob. "An enforcer?"

Dante nodded.

Tipping his chin in acknowledgment, Chissom strode out the door. He turned left and headed into the wing that housed rooms set up for vampires using donors. There were half a dozen bedroom suites, each decorated in a different color, so Chissom knew exactly where Knossis waited.

Reaching the door he needed, Chissom knocked softly, then slipped into the room. He swept his gaze over the space, seeing it empty. The water in the attached bathroom ran, telling Chissom where the shifter was, so he closed the door behind him and waited.

Chissom barely held back a surprised reaction when a

huge, barrel-chested man appeared, freezing a few steps into the room. His light-brown skin was on clear display, since he'd removed his shirt. Dark-brown eyes peered at him warily as he stared back at Chissom.

Lifting his hands, palms out in placation, Chissom introduced himself. "I'm Chissom, and I know you were expecting a woman, but none are available." He saw the way Knossis's full lips tightened and how his brows furrowed, telling him of his displeasure. Chissom guessed a denial was coming and hoped to head it off. Moving a few steps closer, he stated, "I'm sorry you're in pain, Knossis. If you let me, if you share your needs with me, I know I can help you." Smiling a little, showing off his fangs, he assured, "Coming from a vampire bite doesn't have to involve sex."

The tension eased from Knossis's shoulders. "Um, okay." Rubbing a big palm over his bald head, he mumbled, "Haven't had sex in almost a year. Was hopin' . . ."

While Chissom was a switch and would have happily allowed the sexy man to pound his ass, he could tell the uneasy shifter wasn't ready to hear that offer. If Knossis returned after his experience, perhaps he would eventually. Another problem would be the logistics of giving him a good bite, and the neck gave the greatest pleasure, but Chissom doubted Knossis would want to take him from the front so Chissom could reach it.

Maybe I'll bring in a third to help us.

Chissom knew that was a thought for another time. He needed to please the shifter to get him to return . . . and to return to *him*. His mouth watered at the idea of enjoying shifter blood for a few months or more.

Not every vampire enjoyed shifter blood. It was quite a bit bitterer than a human's. On the other hand, it offered a vampire more energy and strength.

Chissom was happy with the tradeoff.

"We can discuss sex another time," Chissom offered, wanting the man to know that it was a future possibility. Moving slowly toward a clearly uncertain Knossis, he smiled in encouragement while adding, "When you're more comfortable with how my bite makes you feel."

After a few seconds, Knossis nodded once.

Pleased, Chissom swept his gaze over Knossis's broad chest. He would love to explore the miles of muscles on the man. Unfortunately, considering he'd expected a woman, he figured the shifter wouldn't welcome his touch just yet.

I hope we can work into it.

"Are there any specific reasons you chose to come here today?" Chissom asked, trying to get the man to share. "Tell me how I can help you, Knossis."

Knossis cleared his throat and nodded. "Did your master tell you my mate isn't available?"

Chissom nodded. "He did, but not specifics." A vampire didn't have the luxury of walking away from their beloved, so he couldn't imagine what Knossis was going through. "Do you want to talk about it?"

Shaking his head, Knossis muttered, "No. I want to get off with someone." He swallowed hard enough to cause his Adam's apple to bob. "I'm tired of my right hand, but I can't keep it up when I'm with someone else, so I was hoping—" Knossis lifted his hand, then dropped it just as quickly.

Nodding once more, Chissom promised, "I can help you with that."

Chissom knew a bonded shifter couldn't get an erection with anyone other than their mate. Since Knossis hadn't claimed his mate, he would struggle, but it could be done. Chissom's bite would be just what he needed.

"Then let's get comfortable," Chissom continued, pointing at Knossis's pants. "I know shifters aren't shy. Do you mind if I strip, too?"

Shrugging one massive shoulder, Knossis told him, "Go for

it." Then he reached for his own fly.

Chissom accepted the permission without comment and crossed to a padded box at the foot of the bed. Sitting, he bent over and pulled off his boots. Rising back to his feet, he made quick work of his clothes, folding them and placing them on the box.

When Chissom turned and spotted a nude Knossis, he sucked in an approving gulp. "Damn, Knoss," he murmured, enjoying the sight of the shifter's smooth chocolate skin, well-proportioned body, and thick muscles. "You are stunning."

The view also had a predictable response on Chissom's body, rousing his prick quickly.

Knossis glanced around the room, clearing his throat awkwardly. "Uh, thanks."

Chissom had no desire to make Knossis uncomfortable, so he moved on quickly. "Come lie down," he urged, pointing at the bed. "Get comfortable."

Nodding, Knossis crossed to it. He hesitated a second, then lay on his back. His dark, flaccid dick nestled against his thighs, and Chissom looked forward to seeing it straining for release.

Easing onto the bed beside Knossis, Chissom stretched out beside him. "Turn on your side, facing away from me," he ordered, resting on his elbow to look down at him. When Knossis's eyes narrowed, Chissom explained, "I'm going to lick and suck on your neck for a few seconds, soaking it in my saliva. That's what will give you maximum pleasure."

Knossis stared at him a moment, even inhaling deeply and openly scenting him. Finally, he rolled away from him.

Chissom slotted up behind Knossis, keeping his lower body well away from the man. Resting his weight on his elbow, he lowered his face to the shifter's shoulder. He placed his right hand on Knossis's hip, lightly teasing his thumb over his hip bone.

Seeing and scenting Knossis's tension, Chissom crooned, "Just relax, Knossis. I can help you."

Then Chissom suckled lightly on Knossis's neck tendon. He scraped his fangs over the flesh before licking and nipping gently. Feeling the tension ease a bit beneath his lips as well as a shiver under his palm, Chissom fought back a smile.

"I'm going to bite you, now, Knossis," Chissom warned against the shifter's neck. "Ready?"

"Y-Yeah," Knossis answered in his deep rough voice.

Chissom eased his fangs into Knossis's flesh, popping through. Hearing Knossis gasp, he suckled. The slightly bitter rush of blood flowed into his mouth, causing his own erection to twitch.

Knossis groaned in Chissom's hold, and Chissom smiled as he drew more blood into his mouth.

Peering down Knossis's broad torso, Chissom watched the shifter's cock swell. He continued to suck as he moved his hand from the male's hip to his dick. Wrapping his fingers around Knossis's engorged length, Chissom jacked him as he fed, giving the man the pleasure he craved.

CHAPTER THREE

"Hey, Chissom," Hank Everly greeted, smiling at the vampire as he put down the book he'd been reading. He admired the vampire's ear-length, sandy-brown hair, reaching up to tuck it behind the friendly wrangler's ear. "How are you?"

Chissom gripped Hank's hand, cupping it with his own. "Doing fine." Turning Hank's wrist, he brought it to his lips and nibbled on the pulse point there. "Better now that I've tracked you down."

Hank snickered even as the hairs on his arm stood on end. For several years, Chissom had fed from Hank as well as a couple of other donors. It had been a couple of months since Chissom had approached him, though, since he'd been feeding from a shifter who visited every week like clockwork.

In fact, Hank was pretty certain it was *that day* for Chissom.

"Tease," Hank murmured, shaking his head. Still smiling, he started to tug at his hand, but Chissom didn't release him. Confused, Hank asked, "What's up?"

"Are you busy this evening?"

Hank shook his head. "I had breakfast dishes duty today, so I'm free."

As a vampire blood donor, Hank essentially worked part-time at the ranch. He also received free room and board as well as a salary. Hank loved the life he'd been leading for the last decade, and at thirty-one years of age, he hoped he could continue there for a long time to come.

"You know I've been seeing a shifter for the last couple of

months, right?"

Smiling, Hank nodded. "Not too many secrets in a vampire coven ranch." He cocked his head, adding, "I just didn't peg you as getting serious and starting a relationship with anyone who wasn't your beloved."

Humming, Chissom settled on the sofa beside Hank, resting their twined hands on his muscled thigh. "Well, it's actually a mutually beneficial arrangement, not a relationship."

Hank gaped. "Really?"

Chissom winked. "I happen to like shifter blood, and Knossis—" He snapped his mouth shut as he glanced around the room. They weren't alone. "Well, his reasons are his own."

"Okay." Hank didn't know what that had to do with him. "Um, is there some way I can help?" he asked, squeezing Chissom's hand.

"I hope so," Chissom replied with a smile. "You like threesomes, right?"

Surprise filling him, Hank felt his blood begin to heat a little at the idea of seeing Knossis in all his naked glory. He'd spotted the big man a couple of times when he was coming and going. While his size and serious expression were a little intimidating, the shifter's muscles made him absolutely drool-worthy.

Chissom chuckled softly as he smirked. "Hmmm, I think you like that idea." As he spoke, he leaned close and tucked his face against Hank's neck, nuzzling lightly as he sniffed him.

Hank moaned softly, tipping his head and offering more room.

Growling, Chissom scraped his fangs along Hank's neck before rumbling, "I've always loved how responsive you are, Hank."

When Chissom pulled away a few seconds later, Hank whimpered with frustration. "Tease," he grumbled. His dick already strained against his fly, and his balls tingled.

Chissom laughed once more as he rose to his feet. "Not a tease," he assured, tugging Hank up with him. Cradling his jaw, he dipped his head and pecked his lips in a swift kiss. "I promise your patience will be rewarded. Come on."

Hank believed Chissom. The vampire had always been a fantastic lover in the past. He looked forward to experiencing Chissom's brand of loving once more.

"Where are we going?" Hank asked curiously when Chissom guided him to the back door.

As Hank toed off his house shoes and pulled on a pair of boots, Chissom told him, "I have a picnic set up at the pond. Knossis is joining us in fox form, so I'll carry you and sprint. Sound okay?"

Nodding, Hank grinned. "That'll be fun."

When a vampire wanted to, they could turn on a burst of speed that rivaled a galloping racehorse. He'd only experienced it once before, and it had been really cool.

Chissom winked before sweeping Hank up bridal style. After he'd stepped off the back deck, and Hank had wrapped his arms around his neck, Chissom took off. The wind whipped by them, the scenery a blur, and Hank laughed as his heart pounded for a new reason—joy.

In a surprisingly short amount of time, Chissom slowed to a walk. He eased Hank to his feet, and he took in the scenery. They'd made it all the way to the pond, and as promised, there was a picnic blanket spread out beside it along with a large basket, a bottle of wine, and a trio of metal goblets.

Chissom took Hank's hand in his own and tucked it into the crook of his elbow. "Come on. Knossis should be here soon. He—"

Just then, the largest red and brown fox Hank had ever seen trotted out of the forest.

"Ah, there he is."

"Wow," Hank whispered in amazement. "He's a big fox."

"He's a big man," Chissom reminded him.

Hank nodded as he watched the fox shift into said man. "Huge," he corrected softly. Then he noticed something in the man's eyes as Knossis glanced from them to the blanket, then around at the setting. "He's sad," Hank whispered. "Why is he sad?"

"He found his mate and can't have her," Chissom told him, keeping his voice low. "That's why he's here. So he can have a sex drive until his fox stops pining for her."

"Oh, damn." Hank's heart tightened in his chest. "That's terrible."

"Don't look at him with pity," Chissom warned.

Hank nodded, pushing down that reaction. "I'm going to milk his cock oh-so-good." Then something else occurred to him. "You're a switch. How come he doesn't want to fuck you?"

Knossis's brows shot up, betraying that he'd heard Hank's question. Grinning unabashedly at the naked enforcer — after all, Hank knew how high a paranormal's sex drive could be — he shrugged. "Just curious." Boldly sliding his gaze over Knossis's gorgeous light-brown body, he focused his attention on the shifter's impressive meat — even while flaccid — and commented, "But I'm not sorry to be the one feeling that slide in and out of my hole."

With his eyes widening, Knossis turned to focus on Chissom. "Chiss? What's he, um" — he cleared his throat awkwardly — "uh, talking about?"

Hank snapped his gaze to Chissom, too. "He didn't know you were inviting me?"

Chissom grinned, focusing on Knossis. Stepping into the shifter's space, he rested his palm on the male's pectoral. Hank saw Chissom tease his thumb over Knossis's nipple and the resulting shiver it caused in the big man.

"We talked about your favorite position while I fed from you," Chissom stated. "How you like me to feed from your neck."

Even though it wasn't a question, Knossis nodded. "Yeah."

"And I bet you're not ready to fuck me face-to-face, so I can easily reach your neck, are you?"

Knossis nibbled his bottom lip, uncertainty clear on his face.

Chissom's smile turned understanding. "It's okay, Knoss," he purred seductively in his smooth tenor. "It just means we bring Hank into the mix." Cutting a hungry expression Hank's way before refocusing on Knossis, Chissom stated, "You'll sink your hard cock into Hank's sweet tight ass. I can tell you from experience, he'll massage your aching length so very good."

When Knossis focused on Hank, his deep brown eyes held a heat that caused butterflies to dance in his belly.

"You'd really let me mount you?"

Taking a chance, Hank lifted a hand and placed it on Knossis's second pectoral, mirroring Chissom. "I would. I'd—"

"So this is where you go every week."

Upon hearing the sneering voice, the trio turned. Chissom and Knossis both stepped forward, placing themselves between the speaker and Hank.

"What are you doing here, Glade?" Knossis demanded. "I'm damn sure you don't have permission to be in coven territory."

Glade curled his lip as he swept his gaze over them. "Don't worry. I won't be here long enough for anyone to notice." His eyes narrowed as he added, "I'm just here to deliver a message."

Knossis crossed his arms over his brawny chest and asked, "What message?"

"That vampires should never have gotten involved in our

skulk business."

In the next instant, a swarm of black bears burst from the trees.

Hank fell back several steps, his mind scrambling as he watched six converge on Knossis and Chissom. He could do nothing to help, and he had no way to defend himself. When another pair ran past the others and attacked him, pain tearing through his body, Hank wished his last memory wasn't of Glade laughing.

CHAPTER FOUR

"I've had it with these damn hunters," Famine roared, slamming his fist on the coffee table. "They're a menace!"

War leaned back on his large sofa and arched one black brow. "Well, if you know where they're hiding, I'd be happy to help you wipe them out."

Famine snarled as he dropped into another chair. "Of course, I don't know where they're hiding." Growling under his breath, he muttered, "Racist pricks."

Rising to his feet, War crossed to his kitchen and pulled a pitcher from a shelf. "How many are you down?" he asked as he grabbed a pair of wooden mugs.

Rubbing his palms over his face, Famine admitted, "Eighteen."

"Shit," War grumbled as he poured mead into each mug. "I've lost twelve demons. All under the age of three hundred," he admitted, returning to the room and holding out one of the mugs to Famine. "They go glamoured and can still be snagged. I've started pairing them up. No demon under the age of five hundred goes to the human realm alone."

After taking a deep swallow of the spiced honeyed mead, Famine shook his head. "I don't have enough older demons to be able to do that and still keep up with the workload the Moirai are asking me to perform."

Famine hated having to admit that, but he'd lost too many demons while infighting with his brothers over the centuries, and his ranks hadn't yet recovered. He figured it was a good thing they'd recently started working together. War's demons were the best trained, and his brother had begun sending his minions to Famine's realm to help train his people.

Which is why I'm here.

Leaning forward, cradling the mug between his palms, Famine swallowed his pride and asked, "On occasion, can one of your older demons escort one of mine?"

War wrapped his large red wings around his shoulders and leaned forward. "I think between the four of us, we should be able to come up with a way to martial our demons to keep them all safe."

Famine nodded before taking a sip of his mead, knowing War referred to the other Horsemen of the Apocalypse—Death and Pestilence.

Before more could be discussed, a loud knock pounded on War's front door. Even before War had gained his feet, the door swung open. War immediately reached for his axe, but seeing who entered, he blew out a breath and shook his head.

"Death, what's wrong?" War asked.

Upon seeing Death's tight features, Famine rose to his feet. Ever since his brothers had started taking partners, he hadn't seen any of them look so upset. Famine didn't know if it was having sex on a regular basis or if it was having a companion, but he'd realized he'd been wrong to sneer at their decision.

"We have a very serious problem," Death stated, scowling. After a nod of hello to Famine, he focused on War. "Do you know Hank and Chissom at Monte's coven?"

Famine knew Monte was one of War's lovers—a vampire, and the second of a coven in Montana. War's other lover was a prairie dog shifter named Xerxes. They were both at the coven while War met with Famine.

War nodded once. "Hank is a human donor. A very sweet and kind man." Resting his hands on his hips, War continued, "Chissom is one of the wranglers. I've only said hello in passing a time or two. Why?"

"They're both about to die." Death crossed his arms over

his slender, robe-covered torso. "And *I* wasn't notified by the Moirai, so I didn't have a demon in place to collect their souls."

"Fuck," War rumbled, his wings lifting from his shoulders, betraying his agitation. "How could this happen? How did you learn of their impending deaths?"

"I heard Hank's final wish and realized who he was due to his location," Death stated, lowering his arms and pivoting. "I have a demon holding their souls, keeping them safe, but I think you should see the scene before I pass them on."

Nodding again, War grabbed his battle axe and hung it from his belt. Famine followed the pair out of War's hut, then through the medieval-style village that made up War's realm. The demon realm was split into four sections, and each was ruled by one of the horsemen. Each brother had decorated their place to their own liking.

When Death and War entered the mists — the gateway that allowed them to travel from the demon realm to the human one — Famine verified the lei line they were using and accompanied them. Upon appearing beside them in a meadow, he saw the surprise on both their faces. He shrugged, saying, "If someone can hide the impending deaths of people from the Moirai, we need to figure out who is doing it and how."

Famine swept his gaze over the area, his focus falling on the carnage. Blood soaked the grass beside a pond where it looked like animals had gutted three bodies, not two. The largest of the lot was nude, although the clothes of the other two hung in tatters, revealing gashes from large claws.

Oddly enough, Famine felt a stirring of . . . something . . . in his gut — sadness, perhaps.

A slender, black demon crouched off to the side, but upon seeing Death, he rose and tipped his head in deference to his master. Between one step and the next, Death's demon disappeared.

"Damn," War muttered softly, shaking his head. "Poor, Hank." He crouched beside the smallest of the trio and touched the human's bloody scalp. "He didn't deserve this."

Death sighed. "None of them did."

War tipped his head up and peered at Death. "I'm detecting faint traces of magick."

Sending out tendrils of his own magick, Famine recognized the signature. "It's the same witches that helped those hunters attack the angel."

"I thought we rounded all of those up?" War countered, rising to his feet.

Famine shrugged. "We must have missed one."

"I scent shifters," Death pointed out.

War pointed at the largest of the victims—a brawny, dark-skinned male. "He's a shifter. Is that who you smell?"

Death shook his head. "No. His name is Knossis and look at the scene." As the horseman who collected souls, Death had the unique ability to know every name of everyone who'd ever lived. Cocking his head, Death stated, "He was trying to help defend Chissom and Hank."

"So, a group of shifters had help from a witch," War mused, his lips tightening. "That's unusual."

"It would take more than one witch to hide deaths from the Moirai," Death claimed, crossing his arms over his chest. "Whoever we missed must have joined a new circle . . . or created one."

"A powerful one," War added.

Death nodded as he whispered, "I wish we could ask them who the shifters were." Then he sighed and knelt beside Hank. "I'll send them on their way."

"Wait," Famine called, stepping closer.

Peering up at him, Death told him, "I can't keep their souls tethered much longer. They need to be allowed to move on."

"I have an idea," Famine countered. Turning to War, he

asked, "You said Hank is a good man, and I'm certain Monte wouldn't allow any vampires but good ones in his coven."

War's brows shot up. "Are you getting at what I think you are?"

Famine nodded once. "You enjoy your companions. Why wouldn't I?"

Death gaped for an instant, then exchanged a look with War. "Are you sure?"

By way of answer, Famine pulled his tunic from his chest. He grunted softly as he unfurled his pale blue wings, allowing them to spring from his shoulder blades. Then Famine knelt before Hank's bloodied head and carefully lifted it onto his lap before wiping his bloody hair from his forehead.

"Hank would bring a lot of joy into your life, Famine," War told him softly. "If you let him, he'll round out your sharp edges."

Snapping his focus to War, Famine scowled at him. "What's that supposed to mean?"

Smirking, Death pointed a finger at him. "That attitude right there." Then he glanced at the shifter. "Will you ask Knossis, too?"

Famine shrugged. "Sure. He's here naked with them, having a picnic." He glanced toward the spread blanket, the picnic basket, and the goblets, which lay pristine in the grass nearby. "I assume he's their lover, so I'll take him, too."

War smirked, crossing his arms over his chest. "Three lovers. This isn't just to one-up the rest of us, is it?"

Grinning broadly, Famine couldn't help but reply, "Maybe just a little."

Death and War chuckled.

"We'll watch your back while you do this," Death promised.

"Thank you."

Famine whispered an ancient spell — one he never thought

he would ever use — and connected his mind to Hank's. Feeling the human's sadness, he felt an odd urge to soothe him. He also felt a fair measure of something he hadn't considered — fear that the human wouldn't accept him.

Hank. Famine whispered into the human's mind. *Can you hear me?*

It took a few sluggish beats of the human's fading heart, but Hank finally responded.

What?

You were gravely injured, Hank. Famine hoped reminding him of whatever had happened didn't bite him in the long run, but he needed to reinforce the gravity of the situation. *Do you remember?*

Yes. Am I dying?

Famine never was one for sugar coating anything. *Yes.* Then he hurried to reassure him. *But you don't have to. Bond with me.*

Who are you?

I am Famine.

War's brother?

Yes. Famine knew he had to share his intention. *I'll ask Chissom and Knossis, too.*

Bond us like Monte and Xerxes are with War?

That's correct.

After a few seconds of waiting — which felt like an eternity, but Famine knew it wasn't — Hank responded with a simple, *Okay.*

Famine sliced open his wrist and urged Hank to drink, all the while trying to understand the hint of giddiness he felt.

CHAPTER FIVE

Knossis's mind drifted in darkness, and he knew he was about to die. He wished he could have at least saved Chissom and Hank. The vampire had been so kind to help him feel again, and to have the man think of a work-around when he couldn't bring himself to fuck another man while facing him . . . so kind.

Damn Glade Whistler. I hope he gets what's coming to him. I wish I could be there to see it happen. I —

Knossis?

Confusion filled Knossis. Had he really heard a voice in his mind?

Knossis? Can you hear me?

Yes? His voice even sounded wary in his mind.

Someone named Glade Whistler did this to you?

Are you Death?

Maybe Knossis would get part of his dying wish, after all. If he could pass on what had happened to them, he could make certain that rat bastard paid.

I am Famine. Death and War are my brothers.

Knossis felt a measure of confusion mixed with fear, which was completely irrational. Sure, he'd met War once before and found him to be a scary motherfucker. Except, really, what could Famine do to him? Knossis was already dying.

How is this possible? What do you want?

Your lovers have agreed to bond with me. If you wish to stay with them, to live, I will bond with you, too.

My lovers. Knossis struggled to sort his thoughts, to understand what could be happening.

Yes. Chissom and Hank. Famine was obviously trying to clarify. *We would all be bound together, sharing each other. Uh, companions and lovers.*

I understand.

During the upheaval in Knossis's skulk, it had come to light who War actually was and how he was bonded with the vampire second, Monte, and a prairie dog shifter named Xerxes. Knossis understood the concept. Except, Knossis had thought dying would be a release from his constant fight against his fox and his desire for his mate.

Do you agree?

If I bond with you, what will happen to my desire to be with my mate? Knossis needed to know upfront. *I don't want to keep fighting these feelings for centuries.*

Knossis didn't know how long a horseman intended to bond for, but he figured it would be for a long damn time.

Famine sounded confused. *If you bond with me, you will still desire Chissom and Hank.* He'd obviously jumped to the wrong idea. *I didn't realize a shifter or vampire could mate in a triad, but it would not change anything between the three of you. I would be added as a fourth, your lifelines continuing through me.*

Knossis gave a mental sigh. *They aren't my mates. I can't have my mate.* He hated how much it hurt every damn time he had to admit that. *She's happily married, and I won't break up that family, not even for Fate.*

Ah, I'm sorry. No, your pull to whoever that woman is will be severed. Famine's growl came through his mind. *It seems whoever is fucking with the Moirai are messing with more than just them passing names on to Death.*

I don't know what that means.

All in good time. After Famine promised that, his tone took on a musing quality. *If you agree to bond with me and decide to live. Your body is about to give out. You must choose.*

Upon hearing the news that Knossis would no longer have to struggle with his fox in regards to a mate they couldn't have, the answer was easy. While Knossis had never been tempted by a male while under ex-alpha Ferris's rule, he couldn't deny he found the idea of spending more time with Chissom and Hank alluring, even after just a few minutes with the latter man. He would be happy to explore more with them.

I choose to live, to bond with you. A malicious thought entered Knossis's mind. *And I can't wait to get my revenge on Glade.*

I would be honored to help. Now drink.

Knossis suddenly realized he felt something at his lips. Obeying, he opened his mouth. His senses told him it was blood even before the spicy flavor hit his taste buds.

Having never claimed a mate, Knossis didn't know if his enjoyment of the flavor of a male who wasn't that to him was normal. He continued to suck on the wound, taking one greedy mouthful after another. His body screamed for more.

As Knossis took another swallow, he realized his dick had grown hard as nails. He moaned around the flesh in his mouth as a tremble worked through him. After one more swallow, Knossis felt his balls tighten, and a wash of tingles erupted over his skin as his orgasm swamped his senses.

"There you go." Famine's voice crooned in his ear, no longer in his head. "Any pain left?"

Licking his lips, Knossis caught his breath. "No," he rasped. Peeling heavy eyelids open, he peered down at himself, and shock filled him. "H-How is this possible?"

Knossis had faced off against three black bears while in human form and naked. The fight had been short and brutal, and he'd known he would lose. He'd sported lacerations that had practically eviscerated his belly and thighs, with a slash that had split open his neck. Now, all Knossis saw was blood-covered skin without a mark in sight.

"The only way to kill a horseman is by beheading," Famine

told him. "And that can only be done by one of our own weapons. We heal from everything else almost instantly." Long slender fingers cradled Knossis's neck, and a thumb under his chin urged Knossis to lift his gaze and meet Famine's for the first time. "And now, so do you."

"Holy shit," Knossis whispered as he stared into the mesmerizing, pale blue eyes and angular features of the Horseman of Famine — the male who'd just saved his life.

But why?

Knossis was a little worried to look a gift horse in the mouth. "You're so very pretty," he mumbled. When both of Famine's nearly white brows shot up, Knossis grimaced, realizing he'd said that out loud. "Sorry." Clearing his throat, he muttered, "Must still be a shortage of blood in my brain."

Famine's thin lips curved into a small smile. "I'm glad you find my features pleasing." The smile faded to be replaced by a slightly furrowed brow. "Some call them cold or haughty."

While Knossis could see how those adjectives could be applied to the man under the right circumstances, he figured something similar could be true of everyone. Most people called him brawny and intimidating. He shook his head, dismissing the absent thoughts and negating Famine's comment all at the same time.

"Do you feel steady enough to stand?" Famine asked, his faint smile returning. It didn't quite meet his ice-blue eyes, as if he had to remind himself to use the expression. "The others are washing in the pond. We should join them."

Knossis turned his head and peered in the direction Famine indicated. His gaze landed on not only an alive and well Hank and Chissom washing in the pond, but on War's hulking form as well as another pale-featured male.

"Who's that?" To Knossis's surprise, he felt a niggle of jealousy that the other men were watching over Hank and Chissom, even if they were talking quietly together and scanning the forest.

Famine followed Knossis's line of sight and told him, "My brothers, War and Death. They've been keeping us safe while I entered your mind to converse with you about bonding." Furrowing his brows just a little, Famine sniffed lightly at him. "Are you upset by their presence?"

Growling softly, Knossis nodded. "They shouldn't see Hank and Chissom naked."

Looking confused, Famine pointed out, "But you are naked." His gaze swept over Knossis's nude body as if checking to make certain that hadn't changed. "Aren't shifters comfortable with nudity?"

"*They* are *not* shifters." Knossis knew he wasn't making much sense, but he couldn't help how he suddenly felt. "And no one should see you naked but us, too."

Famine nodded. "Very well. As soon as you're all clean, I'll clothe you." Rising to his feet, he held out his hand, palm up. "After you all wash."

Knossis took Famine's hand, ready to do whatever it took to get his new lovers clothed, even though he wasn't making much sense, even to himself.

As Knossis headed to the pond to wash, he realized his fox looked forward to spending time with his new men. His animal no longer pined for his mate.

Thank the gods . . . or Famine.

CHAPTER SIX

Chissom cupped his hands and lifted a scoopful of water. Pouring it over Hank's backside, he rinsed the last of the blood away. He gently gripped Hank's shoulder and urged him to turn around to face him.

Seeing Hank's uncertain expression, how he nibbled his plump bottom lip, Chissom cupped his jaw. "What's wrong, Hank?" he asked softly, using his thumb to ease the man's lip free of his teeth. With a smile, Chissom teased, "Only your lovers should nibble on that."

Hank swallowed hard before whispering, "Are you okay with this, Chissom?"

Chuckling softly, Chissom whispered, "Oh, Hank. I really think it's too late to second-guess yourself." He dipped his head and pressed a light kiss to Hank's lips. While it was meant to be reassuring, Chissom still couldn't resist taking a few seconds to dip his tongue into Hank's mouth and enjoy his familiar flavor. Lifting his head, he murmured, "If a vampire had the ability to choose their beloved, you would have been picked a thousand times over." Chissom rubbed his thumb under his human's bottom lip. "While I'm sorry about the circumstances that brought us together, I'm not sorry I get to bond with you, Hank."

Smiling sweetly up at him, Hank whispered, "Thanks." His cheeks pinked a little. "Guess I just needed a little reassurance that you didn't feel railroaded or trapped."

Chissom scoffed softly as he shook his head. "Not at all."

Hearing footsteps, he added, "Life did just get very interesting, however." Chissom focused on the approaching pair, grimacing upon seeing the blood coating Knossis's thick frame. "What do you say you help me clean up Knossis?"

While Chissom worried about the state that Knossis was in, he still admired the differences between the pair. Famine's stately frame actually topped Knossis by a couple of inches. Where Knossis's skin was a medium-brown, Famine was pale. Chissom would bet Knossis's hair — if he chose to grow it — would have been dark-brown or black, while Famine's slicked-back, shoulder-length hair was a pale blond. Even their eyes were opposite — dark-brown and light-blue.

"You're looking at us like you're sizing up your next meal."

Famine's comment pulled Chissom out of his perusal of the pair that had suddenly become his permanent lovers. "Sorry." He chuckled as he stepped forward, reaching for Knossis. "Just admiring you both." Gripping the big man's wrist, Chissom tugged him into the water. "Care to strip, Famine?" With a wink, he added, "Hank and I are going to wash Knossis, and we'd love for you to join us."

"Go play in the water, brother," War called, amusement lacing his tone. "We'll go scout the area."

Death didn't look their way, but he did wave. "See you in an hour. Start your bonds quick."

Knossis growled softly as he glared in War and Death's direction, but the pair were already disappearing amidst the trees.

"Relax, Knossis," Hank encouraged, gripping the shifter's other wrist, drawing him deeper into the water. "I'm guessing you're feeling pretty territorial right now because our bonds aren't complete."

Chissom grinned, seeing the wisdom in Hank's words. "You're absolutely right," he stated with a nod. "Let's get you cleaned up so we can get back to the fun we'd planned earlier this evening." Releasing Knossis, Chissom turned to Famine, who still stood on the shore, and started toward him. "Time to disrobe, Famine. Come join your lovers."

For an instant, Famine appeared taken aback by Chissom's directness. He didn't let that stop him. After all, the horseman would have to get used to their ways.

Resting his palms on Famine's hips, Chissom teased his thumbs under the hem of the lean man's tunic. He traced over his muscular hip bones for an instant, gratified upon seeing the way Famine's eyes dilated while the blue darkened a smidge. Chissom also scented the sweet muskiness of arousal.

"Lift your arms, Famine," Chissom urged, guiding the tan tunic upward. When the horseman seemed frozen, he rumbled huskily, "Don't make me grow my claws and shred these handsome clothes from your body."

Chissom would do it, although he would hate to do so. The tunic and form-fitting, light-brown leather pants fit Famine's body like a glove. They accentuated every line of the horseman's regal — if a bit tense — frame.

When Famine still didn't respond, Chissom used one hand to grip the soft fabric of the horseman's shirt. He lifted his free hand and spread his fingers. Then he slowly grew his claws, unsheathing his three-inch talons, and wiggled his fingers.

"Last chance to save that shirt," Chissom warned, suddenly anticipating stripping his soon-to-be lover, one way or another. He could hear Hank and Knossis behind him and the splash of water. "Can't wait to see you naked. To play with the others."

Chissom touched his claws to where he'd bunched Famine's shirt. That seemed to snap Famine out of whatever had held him in thrall.

Famine gripped Chissom's wrist in a firm hold, staying his action. "I'll keep my tunic, thanks." After easing Chissom's talons a few inches from his clothing, he smiled. "I just might enjoy feeling those scrape over my body someday."

"They feel amazing," Hank called, having obviously been paying attention to them. He waggled his eyebrows. "You'll love it."

Humming, Famine whipped his tunic over his head. "Then I look forward to it." He reached for the stays on his leather pants. "Now go clean our lover. I want to run my palms over everyone's skin as soon as you're finished."

Chissom narrowed his eyes as he read into what Famine wasn't saying. The horseman didn't intend to join them in the water.

Well, fuck that.

Turning as if to obey, Chissom watched from the corner of his eye as Famine focused on his pants. He planted his feet, twisted while bending his knees, and grabbed the unsuspecting horseman around the waist. Then he heaved up and sideways, jumping at the end of the move.

Chissom heard Famine's bark of surprise just before the water of the pond crashed over them both. Anticipating retaliation, he came up fast. He knew that men as powerful as Famine wouldn't take kindly to being thrown around like that.

I also hope that since I'm half-bonded with him — having drank Famine's delectable blood to heal — *it'll earn me some leniency.*

"What the fuck!" Famine roared as he broke the surface and stood.

Even as Chissom admired the way the water trickled down Famine's pectorals, he recognized the anger blazing within the horseman's blue eyes. He decided to go on the offensive. Stepping forward, Chissom grabbed Famine's upper arm and got right up in his space.

"We may not be beloveds by Fate, but we are working on a bond." Chissom held Famine's anger-filled eyes and added, "That means until we've completed the bonds between us all, we do things together." Seeing the way Famine's eyes narrowed, Chissom softened his tone as he moved his hold up the horseman's arm to his shoulder so he could massage the tense tendon there. "And if you give us a chance, you may even find that you like it."

Famine's nostrils flared, and his eyes narrowed. A tick formed in his jaw. He lifted his chin, as if he were ready to deny Chissom, maybe even yell at him.

"Please, Famine?" Hank spoke up softly from where he stood beside Knossis. "It'd be a nice way to get to know each other as we have a little fun."

Chissom couldn't help but notice how a half-cleaned Knossis held his thick arm around Hank's shoulders—which were a bit tight with tension—in a clearly supportive and protective gesture. His dark eyes held a hint of concern. Knossis seemed to be waiting with bated breath.

For some reason, Chissom just knew their future hinged on how Famine responded to their request.

Famine swept his gaze over them. His nostrils flared, and he snapped his attention to Hank.

Ah, he's scented it, too. Hank's unease, his concern, and yes, his fear.

After a swallow so hard his Adam's apple bobbed, Famine let out a deep sigh. "Please forgive my anger," he murmured, his tenor soft and melodic. "It has"—he drew out his words slowly, as if choosing each one carefully—"been a long time since someone has ignored my . . . order." Famine focused on Chissom. "Or had the audacity to counter it."

Chissom did a quick calculation of his options—to apologize, call the man on his shit, or defer. Knowing how important open communication in any relationship was, he decided to do a little of all three.

"I'm not sorry for dunking you," Chissom told him with a smile. As Famine's brows began to arch, he hurried to add, "We need to start doing things together, learning how to be partners, and staying out of things that should be done to-gether won't build a solid foundation between us." Using a bit of vampiric strength, Chissom used his hold on Famine's shoulder—while stepping closer to the horseman's side—to turn the male in Knossis's direction. "Now, how about we *all* finish cleaning up our shifter. Then we can enjoy that picnic I packed by the pond?"

While Chissom knew he would need to report to Master Dante about the attack soon enough—hell, War had probably already told Monte through their mental bond—he knew con-necting with his trio of men was even more important.

My master will understand.

CHAPTER SEVEN

R elief flooded Hank when Famine relaxed. The anger he'd felt through their unfinished bond had shocked him—not only with its intensity, but with the fact that he was able to feel it at all. Hank wondered just how powerful their link would end up between them.

Reaching out to Hank, Famine gently cradled his nape. "I didn't mean to upset you, my human." His pale brows furrowed, and his eyes narrowed. "This will"—he waved his free hand, indicating all of them—"take some getting used to."

Hank nuzzled into Famine's palm. "I understand," he assured, smiling at him through his lashes. "Change is hard, no matter the reason." He shivered as he thought about what had brought them together. "Especially when it's traumatic."

Famine must have caught on to Hank's thoughts, for he wrapped his free arm around him and pulled him close. Flushing their wet bodies together, he tucked Hank to his chest. Famine dipped his head and pressed a kiss to the top of his head.

"Think not on the beasts who attacked you," Famine crooned into his ear. "My brothers and I will track and destroy them."

"We should start by talking to Glade," Knossis interjected with a growl. He cracked his knuckles, and with a dark smile, he added, "I can't wait to see his reaction when I return to skulk lands."

"You will *not* be put in danger," Famine declared, which totally ruined their bonding moment, and Hank grimaced where his face was pressed against the horseman's side.

Knossis scowled, crossing his arms over his chest. "I'm an enforcer," he declared. "Danger sorta comes with the territory."

"No," Famine stated again, his body tight with tension against Hank's own. He peered around at everyone. "None of you should ever be in danger again."

Chissom stepped close, settling one hand on Famine and Knossis's upper arms. "I saw War go through this with Monte." He smiled as he glanced between them. "We all come from separate lives, but we'll learn to work through our differences."

Hank appreciated Chissom being the voice of reason. Unable to help himself, he piped up, "And I really wanna ask Glade where he got the bears. Were they shifters?"

"They were," Chissom confirmed. "And we'll get to that." He swept his gaze over a naked and only half-clean Knossis. "Let's finish what we started, lovers."

More than on board with that, Hank eased from Famine's hold. Bending, he cupped a handful of water and swept it up Knossis's left leg. To Hank's delight, he saw Knossis shiver under his touch . . . and it wasn't all due to the cold pond water. The shifter's dick twitched oh-so-near to Hank's face as he continued to rinse the blood from Knossis's leg, cleaning away the traces of the attack.

Hank licked his lips, and his mouth watered. He couldn't wait to taste his soon-to-be lover. His own prick twitched in anticipation, even while in the chilly pond.

Chissom joined Hank, crouching to clean Knossis's other leg. Famine watched them for a couple of heartbeats before moving closer, stopping behind Knossis. He bent and scooped up water, dripping it over the shifter's lower back.

Knossis blew out a rough breath, his fingers twitching

where they hung at his sides. "Gods, I can't believe I'm getting hard from this," he muttered, his voice deep and rough. "But your touches . . . they're better than anything I've ever felt before." Confusion flooded his tone. "Why?"

Famine rubbed his hands up his back and rumbled into Knossis's ear, "You can feel my connection to Hank and Chissom through the bond we share, Knossis." Nipping at the shifter's neck, he continued, "We may not have been your original mate, but we are now. Our touches will always enflame your blood."

Sighing, Knossis tipped his head to the side, offering Famine more room. "I like that."

At the simple response, Hank smiled. "Me, too." He rubbed his wet hands up Knossis's side as he rose to his feet. "Almost all clean. Just one more spot."

"Where?" Famine asked, peering down Knossis's body. "Ah."

A wicked grin curved Chissom's lips as he cupped water and rose to his feet. "Here." Then he wrapped his wet hands around Knossis's half-hard prick, rinsing him and jacking him all at once.

Knossis groaned and bucked into his hold. "Damn. Feels even better than before," he muttered, perhaps referring to the many times he and the vampire had been together over the weeks. "More."

"Oh, you'll get more," Chissom promised, even as he released him. "Out of the water. You still want to fuck Hank, right?"

Knossis focused on Hank, a hungry gleam in his dark eyes. "Oh, yes."

Heat flushed through Hank's body. "Yes, please," he answered breathily, glancing down at Knossis's thick erection. The shifter's shaft was in proportion to his body — huge. Hank guessed that, if he were to measure the man, he would be a good ten inches with a thick girth. "Oh, yes."

Growling, Knossis gripped Hank's wrist and turned, heading out of the water.

Chissom chuckled, wrapping his arm around Famine's waist. "I'd really like to see what you're packin'," he claimed. "Because these wet leather pants are telling me it'll be amazing."

Hank lowered his gaze to Famine's groin even as he allowed Knossis to lead him from the water. Upon seeing the long, slender length obscenely cradled by the wet pants, he moaned softly. He felt his chute muscles clench in anticipation. While Hank wasn't completely sure, he would guess that Famine was even longer than Knossis, albeit slenderer.

Knossis must have followed Hank's gaze, for he muttered, "Damn, Famine." Sounding confused, he asked, "Why do I suddenly want to feel that in my ass? I've never wanted a guy to fuck me before."

"You may be picking up on my desires," Hank offered, glancing at Famine for confirmation.

"And mine." Chissom cupped Famine's crotch, blatantly fondling his length. "Because I can't wait to feel Famine long-dicking me with this rod."

Famine groaned, bucking his hips. "Yessss," he hissed. "Hank is right." His blue eyes warmed, revealing his desire as he stared into Chissom's eyes. "And I'll give you exactly what you need, my vampire."

Chissom grinned widely, showing off his fangs. "Looking forward to it."

They stopped at the blanket, and while Chissom began working on Famine's pants, Hank noticed Knossis's sudden case of nerves. While the big shifter still sported a huge erection, he didn't make a move to do anything. He glanced from Hank to the blanket to Chissom and Famine and back again.

Hank rested his palms on Knossis's chest and slid one up

to touch the shifter's jaw. "Hey." Once his soon-to-be lover peered down at him, Hank asked, "What's wrong?"

Knossis licked his lips, then swallowed hard enough to cause his Adam's apple to bob. "I-I've never done this before," he whispered gruffly. "I don't know what to do."

Understanding dawned as Hank remembered why he'd joined Chissom in the first place. Smiling softly, he rubbed his forefingers along Knossis's jaw lightly. "I'll show you how to stretch a lover," he told him. "Just relax on the blanket and watch." With a wink, Hank added, "And if you decide you want to join in, that's fine, too."

"No, I think *we'll* do that for you," Famine countered, drawing Hank's attention.

Sucking in a sharp breath at the regal figure the damp-skinned male made, Hank stared as a fresh wash of desire crashed through his system.

Famine chuckled, his smile turning feral. "Yesss. That's the kind of looks I've been missing." He looked at Chissom. "Get the lube. I'll open you and Hank up while you both play with Knossis's dick."

Chissom grinned broadly, showing off his fangs. "Fantastic idea." He dropped to his knees on the blanket and pulled a tube of lube out of the front pocket of the basket. "Lie down in the middle, Knossis," he ordered, popping the cap. "It's time to give your gorgeous piece of meat the attention it deserves."

Knossis only hesitated an instant before lowering his hulking form to the blanket.

Hank and Chissom quickly followed him down, each kneeling on either side of his hips. While Chissom handed the slick to Famine, who knelt near Knossis's feet, Hank rested his hand on their shifter's tight abdominals.

"Just relax back," Hank encouraged, pressing lightly. "We'll take excellent care of you."

Furrowing his brows, even as he obeyed, Knossis muttered, "I'm supposed to take care of you."

As Hank rubbed his hand over Knossis's expansive torso, he asked, "Why?"

"Well, because I'm bigger than you," Knossis stated slowly before his breathing hitched. Hank glanced down, noticing Chissom rubbing the backs of his fingers up and down Knossis's straining erection. "And a sh-shifter."

Chuckling softly, Hank shook his head. "Well, when it comes to sex, we won't be having those sorts of distinctions."

To reinforce his words, Hank tweaked Knossis's nipple, pleased to see it tighten under his ministrations. He continued working it as he bent over and blew a breath over the shifter's cock head. Seeing the bead of pre-cum bubbling from the slit made Hank's mouth water.

After a glance at Chissom, who seemed focused on mouthing Knossis's balls while working his other nipple, Hank stuck out his tongue and swiped it over the shifter's flared head.

Knossis barked a deep cry, so Hank went back for more.

Chapter Eight

Famine popped the cap on the lube as he watched Hank and Chissom play with Knossis. The way the shifter's dark, engorged length jumped, jerked, and leaked pre-cum caused Famine's mouth to water. He couldn't remember the last time he'd sucked cock, but for his new lovers — *my companions* — he knew he would eventually.

While Chissom had shocked the hell out of Famine when he'd tossed him in the water, he had to admit that he admired the vampire's tenacity. Famine hadn't seen the move coming. He also appreciated that his lovers were willing to stand up to him.

Offering someone equality in a relationship would definitely take some getting used to, but Famine wanted this to work, so he would figure it out.

At least I know one of them will call me on it when I fuck up.

Famine wouldn't delude himself. He wasn't perfect. Having never been in a relationship, he would at some point.

Chissom lifted his head from where he was suckling Knossis's balls and peered at Famine with a heavy-lidded, hazel-eyed gaze. "Is something wrong, Famine?"

Smiling faintly, Famine shook his head. "Just admiring the view."

Offering a roguish grin, Chissom told him, "Admire while stretching our asses." He winked, continuing, "Because my chute is desperate to milk your cock."

Groaning softly, Famine ordered, "Get your asses over here."

As Hank and Chissom obeyed, swinging their asses more to face him while Chissom went back to suckling Knossis's balls, Famine poured a dollop of lube over the fingers of one hand, then the other. He closed the tube and set it aside. Reaching out, he ran a slippery finger down the trench of both his new lovers.

In response, Hank arched his back and moaned around the dick head he suckled.

Chissom grunted while shifting his legs wider.

Famine hummed appreciatively, enjoying their responses. As Hank's chute easily gave way, telling him the human was a natural bottom, Chissom's star offered a bit more resistance. For just an instant, Famine wondered when the vampire had last bottomed before realizing it didn't matter.

He's mine now.

That possessive thought was new to Famine, but it still lodged a pleasant burn in his gut.

Eager to seal the deal, Famine began working both men open in earnest. He reveled in their grunts and moans, which transferred to Knossis's groin. That drew hisses and shudders from the big shifter, sweat breaking out on his chest and brow.

The fragrant aroma of masculine need filled the air, driving Famine's arousal even higher. He reveled in the heated clench on the two fingers in Chissom and the three in Hank. His erection jerked at his groin, eager to move forward.

Chissom popped off Knossis's balls, looked back at Famine, and growled, "I'm ready, damn it." His irises were red, betraying his need. "Need you now."

"One more finger for Hank," Famine countered, pushing a fourth finger into the mentioned man. "Knossis is big."

Grimacing, Chissom nodded.

Hank released the shifter's massive erection. Panting harshly, he claimed, "I'm ready. I love the burn of the stretch." He grinned, his brown eyes gleaming as he stared at Knossis's saliva-drenched cock. "And Knossis's shaft is going to stretch me so good."

With his dick aching, Famine was happy to take Hank at his words. He eased his fingers out of each man. While wiping one hand on the blanket, Famine grabbed his own shaft with the other, slicking himself up.

With his chest heaving, Knossis rumbled, "H-How do we d-do this?"

Knossis's fingers were twisted in the blanket, and his abdominals were clenched tight. With wild eyes, he stared at Hank. He appeared ready to pounce on the human and was barely holding himself back.

"Climb onto Knossis's waist," Famine ordered. For some reason, he wanted to push his shifter lover's control. "Ride him, Hank."

Hank glanced at Famine with a heavy-lidded gaze as he nodded. Nibbling his bottom lip, he rose up and swung one leg over Knossis's thick waist. Famine gripped his hips, helping to steady him as Chissom grabbed the base of the shifter's swollen erection.

Famine looked over Hank's shoulder and spotted Knossis's glazed eyes staring at Hank's groin. At first, he thought he was staring with anticipation. Then Famine noticed something else in Knossis's eyes—nerves.

"Knossis," Famine crooned. When that didn't get his shifter's attention, he gently ordered, "Knossis, look at me."

After blinking once, Knossis focused on Famine. "Are you okay?"

Knossis's brows furrowed. He opened and closed his mouth, but no words came out. He didn't seem to know how to respond.

Chissom rubbed Knossis hip and asked, "What are you thinking? Is it the face-to-face thing?" Before Famine could question the vampire's meaning, he glanced at Famine and quietly told him, "Knossis has never fucked a guy before."

A bolt of shock filled Famine . . . until he remembered that Knossis had referred to a mate—a female mate. "Ah." He focused back on the still-stunned-looking shifter. "Should we change positions?"

Finally, Knossis seemed to gather himself enough to shake his head. "No, just." He stared at Hank's groin again before looking at the human's face. "Your hole is so small, and I'm so huge. How could it possibly feel good to you?"

Famine could just make out the corner of Hank's understanding smile. "Oh, Knossis," he crooned. Resting his palms on the shifter's torso, he teased at his swollen nipples. "I'm a natural bottom. I love the stretch and burn." Leaning down, Hank pressed a chaste kiss to the corner of Knossis's mouth, which caused the scent of the shifter's surprise to perfume the air. Rising back up, Hank purred, "I want to feel your erection splitting me open so very much. Will you let me?" Then he bumped his ass against Knossis's crown.

Knossis groaned, and his hips jerked. "Yes," he rasped on a moan. "Oh, gods, please do something. I-I need s-so fucking badly."

"We know what you need," Chissom rumbled. "Relax and enjoy."

With his hold still on Hank's hips, Famine began to guide the human down. He helped him press his opening firmly to Knossis's cock head, and he watched the well-prepared opening expand and swallow his shifter's swollen flesh. Hank moaned, and Famine paused, but his human shook his head.

"More," Hank urged. "So good."

Famine obeyed, helping Hank lower himself the rest of the way down in one long glide.

Knossis gritted his teeth, a muscle jumping in his jaw. His chest rose and fell in swift panting breaths. His abdominals clenched, and a low, growly moan fell from his lips.

Smiling over Hank's shoulder, Famine murmured, "Feel

how tight that is around your cock, Knoss?" He saw the way Knossis's eyes were dilated so wide, the black dominating, and urged, "Lift a bit, Hank. Give him a squeeze."

Hank did as ordered, lifting halfway off Knossis's cock, then sinking back down.

Knossis tipped his head back and roared his bliss.

Famine's erection jerked at the ecstasy-filled sound, and he groaned as his own need roared through him. Easing backward, he gripped Chissom's hand. "Help guide him, my vampire, as I take you."

Chissom's nostrils flared, and his eyes once again hazed to red. The vampire's need had faded somewhat while soothing their shifter's nerves. Now, he grinned and nodded, just as eager to get in on the play.

Positioning Chissom behind Hank between Knossis's slightly spread calves, Famine slotted up behind him. As Chissom rested one hand on the shifter's thigh for balance, he placed his other on Hank. Then Famine pressed his cock head to Chissom's hole, and a shiver of anticipation coursed up his spine.

"Mine," Famine declared, thrusting into the vampire.

Chissom groaned as his passage opened to Famine, swallowing him in blessed heat. "Yours," he confirmed, much to Famine's delight.

Famine gripped Chissom's hips, pulling him closer until he rested on his lap. Buried deep in the other man, he panted softly. His erection throbbed insistently, but Famine ignored it as his mind flew on the knowledge that he was completing his bond with Chissom.

I'll do this soon enough with the others, too.

For several seconds, Famine relished the heat and squeeze along his length. He couldn't imagine why he'd allowed himself to have such a dry spell. His duties had seemed so important, but he should have found time to relax, to find pleasure.

To Famine's surprise, Chissom peered over his shoulder at him and gave him a feral smile. "Don't worry. We won't allow you to have that long of a dry spell again."

"How?" Then it hit Famine. "We already have a mind link?"

How is that possible when we hadn't yet finished our bond?

Chissom smiled and shrugged one shoulder. "Not sure, but I heard from Monte that it happened to him and War, too."

Famine processed that for all of two seconds before he decided on something. "That's interesting, but we shouldn't be talking about my brother while having sex."

Barking a laugh, Chissom nodded. "Then fuck me, Famine."

Famine was only too happy to obey.

CHAPTER NINE

When Hank had first lowered himself onto his erection, Knossis had nearly blown his load right that second. Chissom and Hank had played with his body, had ramped up his need so damn much that he'd nearly torn a hole in the blanket. With Hank's hot body wrapped around his cock, Knossis did just that.

Clenching his abdominals, a hard shudder working through him, Knossis barely held back the urge to buck his hips. Instead, his arms jolted. The rending of fabric filled the air, but before Knossis could draw enough brain cells together to apologize, Hank began moving.

Hank's tight chute muscles massaged his length with each move Hank made. His balls were already screaming for release, and he didn't know how much longer he could control himself. He desperately wanted to touch his lover, but with Hank being a human, Knossis feared his own strength.

"Hey," Hank crooned, leaning over him, his weight on his hands where they rested on Knossis's chest. "You okay?"

Knossis wished his lovers would stop asking him that. Licking his lips, he nodded. "Just" —Hank eased up a little, then back down, yanking a low growl from his throat—"d-don't w-want to h-hurt—" When Hank did it again, Knossis lost his train of thought.

Hank must have gotten the idea. "You won't." He sounded so sure of himself. Then he settled his ass on Hank's groin and ground against him, while clenching and releasing his chute muscles. "Fuck me, Knoss."

Losing all control, Knossis could do little else. He released the blanket and gripped Hank's hips. Feeling another's hand already on one, he slid that one up to Hank's side. Then Knossis lifted the small human up a little, halfway off his aching erection, and took over.

Knossis stared at his cock as he began bucking his hips. The sight of his dick appearing and disappearing from Hank's body set his blood aflame almost as much as the exquisite feel of it. His fox roared with his need to mark and claim, driving him on to rut faster and faster.

"That's the way, Knossis," Chissom rumbled breathily. "Pound Hank's lush ass. Make him feel you owning it, owning him."

Tearing his gaze away from the spectacular sight of him reaming his lover, Knossis met Chissom's red-eyed gaze over Hank's shoulder. The vampire nuzzled Hank's neck, licking and sucking along his tendon. Knossis could just see Famine doing the same to the other side of Chissom's neck, a look of feral delight on the horseman's face. With the way the pair jolted just a little, Knossis realized Famine had to be fucking Chissom, hard and fast.

Even as Knossis relished the feel of Hank's hot, squeezing body, his chute muscles clenched. He met Famine's gaze over his lover's shoulders. Somehow, Knossis knew that Famine intended to do that to him, and soon, and he realized he looked forward to it.

When the hand on Hank's hip reached for Knossis's and twined their fingers, he realized it was his vampire's hand. Knossis's heart swelled, as somehow, he felt as if the touch drew them all together as one.

The touch also had the benefit of sending an extra burst of heat through his limbs. A tingle settled in his balls, and he knew he was seconds away from coming. He groaned and, squeezing Chissom's fingers, thrust deep into Hank and held it there.

His orgasm surged through him, and he unloaded, coating his new mate with his release.

To Knossis's shocked satisfaction, Hank tipped his head back and howled his pleasure as the human's erection erupted. His lover's cum splashed over Knossis's torso, fragrant and mouth-watering. His fox urged him to taste . . . something else.

Acting on instinct, Knossis wrapped his arm around Hank's waist and jerked him closer. Crunching his abs, he wrapped his jaw around the point of the human's shoulder opposite where Chissom had been sucking. Knossis felt his canines extend, just as if Hank was his true mate, and he gave in to the urge to sink them into the human's flesh.

Knossis groaned when Hank's iron-rich life-fluid flowed across his tongue. His fox howled in his mind as he swallowed first one mouthful, then a second. He felt something in his mind — some tether he'd never before experienced — slide into place, giving him a sense of peace he'd never felt before.

Moaning at the sensation as well as the taste, Knossis felt his cock pulse an extra burst of cum. Easing his teeth free of Hank's neck, he licked the blood away. To his surprise, a claiming mark remained.

Holy shit! I just claimed my mate.

Joy flooded him.

"Ease out, Knoss," Chissom urged huskily. "I need Hank."

Even though leaving the warm cocoon of Hank's body was the last thing Knossis wanted to do, he spotted the tortured expression on Chissom's face and obeyed. He gently lifted Hank's hips, allowing his erection to slip free. As Knossis watched, his vampire stared at Hank's ass as if it were a steak and he was starving.

With Hank still draped over his chest, Knossis could feel his human's moan when Chissom sank his thick, red erection into Hank's ass. He watched in fascination as Chissom fucked his mate. Amazement coupled with lust flooded him without a hint of jealousy. Instead, Knossis wondered what the vampire's cock felt like.

"Gods, Hank," Chissom mumbled, his eyes red with passion and lust. "So fucking good."

"Now, Chissom," Famine demanded from where he still fucked Chissom. "Come now. Mark our human just as our shifter did."

Knossis watched with a growing throb in his still-hard cock as Chissom obeyed. The vampire sank his fangs into Hank's neck, causing the human to cry out. At the same time, Famine sank surprisingly sharp-looking canines into Chissom's neck and stilled, all the while staring into Knossis's eyes.

Soon.

Knossis felt certain he heard the whispered vow in his mind.

Then Famine broke their gaze and focused on the flesh he sucked.

Chissom moaned and pulled his lips free of Hank's neck. Blood dripped from his fangs, and he shuddered. Then he licked at Hank's flesh, cleaning and sealing the mark he'd left.

For some reason, seeing the twin claiming scars on Hank's neck set Knossis's blood on fire. When Famine pulled his teeth free, revealing a scar on Chissom, Knossis's cock throbbed. His fox growled in his mind, and a desperate need to see his own mark on Chissom's neck surged through him.

As soon Famine eased back a little, Chissom groaned and slipped to the left. Chuckling, Famine remained on his knees, revealing he still sported a long, slender erection. The organ jerked and twitched as the horseman focused on Hank. Sliding his arms around the human's torso, Famine pulled their lover onto his lap, his ass to Famine's crotch. With a quick lift to Hank and a shift of his hips, Famine slid his erection into Hank's dripping hole.

Feeling his own cock continue to ache, Knossis groaned

and palmed his still-slick shaft.

"Need help with that?" Chissom murmured, sliding his hand up Knossis's thigh.

Knossis focused on Famine's mark on Chissom's neck. Growling, he half-rolled, allowing him to grab his vampire's waist. He dragged Chissom flush to his chest, then rolled, laying his lover beneath them.

"Yes," Knossis hissed. "Need you."

To Knossis's relief, Chissom wrapped his arms around his shoulders as he spread his legs. He rocked his hips, pressing against Knossis's erection.

"Take me," Chissom encouraged.

Knossis couldn't have resisted Chissom's plea even if the whole world was coming down around him. With a shift of his hips, he found the vampire's opening and pushed. Feeling Chissom's muscles give way, his prick became enveloped in silky heat and pressure, and a low growl of bliss erupted from him.

Unable to help himself, Knossis eased nearly all the way out, only to push right back in again.

"Oh, Knoss," Chissom whispered into his ear, rocking into his thrusts. "Wanted to feel your gorgeous cock in my ass so many times." He moaned and trembled in Knossis's hold. "B-Better than I could ever imagine."

"Wondered how you'd feel," Knossis admitted. He had, too, in the dark of the night when he was all alone. Even though Knossis had known that all he would have to do is ask, he'd never been able to force his tongue to say the words. "So good, Chiss."

"And yours," Chissom reminded, then groaned low in his throat. "Fuck, yeah. Right there."

Knossis obeyed, nailing Chissom's prostate over and over. The look of sheer bliss on his vampire's face sent a wave of heady satisfaction through Knossis. He relished pleasing the more experienced male and sped up his strokes.

"Ah, fuck! Knoss!"

Chissom crying his name was music to Knossis's ears. That coupled with the squeeze of his lover's chute as he orgasmed yanked Knossis right over the edge with him. His balls pulled tight, and he emptied into Chissom's body.

With his fox urging him on, Knossis sank his canines into a second person for the night. He moaned as he drank Chissom's warm, rich blood. When he felt his vampire convulse again and smelled another burst of seed, Knossis poured several extra pulses into his lover.

CHAPTER TEN

Chissom panted softly as he floated on wave after wave of endorphins. As he came back to himself, he registered the petting of several sets of hands. He smiled as he peeled open eyelids he didn't remember closing.

Hank lay to his left. Famine sprawled on his right. Knossis continued to lie on top of him, although he had most of his weight on his elbows. The shifter hung his head, pressing his forehead just below where he'd bitten Chissom, seemed to be as far as Knossis managed to move.

His other lovers petted both him and Knossis, soothing them.

"Damn," Chissom mumbled, struggling to get his mushy brain to formulate words. With a chuckle, he slurred, "Never experienced a marathon like that."

Famine growled softly, his blue eyes sparkling. "Almost done," he told him. "You just lie there and enjoy the feel of Knossis's hard dick in your ass as I fuck him and complete our connections."

Lifting his head took the last of his coordination, but Chissom managed it. His eyes widened with his surprise when he saw Hank expertly opening Knossis's ass. With the way the shifter shuddered atop him, Chissom just bet that their experienced human used every trick in the book to pleasure Knossis as he stretched him.

Hank met Chissom's gaze and smiled before winking.

A second later, Knossis groaned and shuddered.

Chissom took his cue and squeezed his chute muscles.

"Fuck!" Knossis whined. "Oh, gods."

"Not a god," Famine crooned into his ear. "But close." Then he eased into position between both Chissom and Knossis's legs. "Relax." He rubbed his palms down Knossis's broad back until he palmed the shifter's cheeks. "This won't take long, my shifter. I'm so very primed after claiming our lovers."

As Chissom watched, Famine sank his long, hard dick into Knossis's body. Even with all the prep, their shifter still tensed. Famine grimaced and froze as Hank teased his fingers beneath them, probably to play with Knossis's balls.

Wanting to do his part, Chissom clenched and released his inner muscles. He massaged his lover's erection, stimulating him as best as he could. When Knossis grunted, Chissom knew he was on the right track and continued his efforts.

After a few more seconds, Knossis relaxed in their ministrations. He sighed deeply and moaned into Chissom's neck. Massaging his shifter's shoulder blades, he felt each thrust Famine made as Knossis twitched above him.

In a surprisingly short amount of time, Knossis hissed and tensed.

Chissom rubbed his palms down Knossis's back, urging, "Don't fight it, our shifter. Come for your lovers."

Whining, Knossis obeyed. His big body convulsed, and Chissom felt the hard dick in his chute jerk and twitch. The heat of Knossis's seed warmed him from the inside out, telling him without words that their shifter had come.

Then Famine struck, biting Knossis's neck with canines that resembled fangs.

Knossis shuddered again, and Chissom smiled, knowing exactly what his lover was feeling. Famine's bite had been damn fantastic, causing him to come again. When Knossis's elbows slid out from under him, landing his full weight on Chissom, he barely resisted gasping.

Instead, Chissom wrapped his arms around Knossis and rubbed up and down his back. He nuzzled the shifter's neck over his claiming scar, which was opposite where Famine continued to suckle. After a moment, Knossis groaned softly and shifted his head a little.

"Holy fucking shit," Knossis mumbled, his words a little garbled since his face was still pressed to Chissom's chest. "H-How is that even possible?"

Chissom's brain, still a little sluggish, didn't follow. "What's that?" he asked as he continued to pet Knossis's muscular sides. Occasionally, his hands bumped against Hank's, telling him their human did his best to soothe, too. Hank's other hand seemed to be stroking Famine, so Chassis reached a little further and did the same, enjoying the opportunity to touch the horseman, who he guessed was normally pretty uptight.

I'll help him work on that.

Famine lifted his head and smirked at him. *Will you?*

Chuckling, Chissom winked. *Yup. Still getting used to having to control if I'm broadcasting my thoughts.*

Fortunately, Famine responded by sending a warm chuckle echoing through his mind.

"Getting off from something stuck up your ass," Knossis answered bluntly. When he turned his head, he briefly met Chissom and Hank's gazes before staring at Chissom's nipple while muttering, "It should have hurt more."

"That's what prep does for you," Hank told him. Their human lay on his side, his leg over theirs as he petted everyone's skin on that side. "You prepare your lover, stretch them and tease their prostate, so when you do enter them, it doesn't hurt."

"But you talked about liking a burn." Knossis sounded confused. "Why would you like that, um . . . there?"

Chissom noticed a hint of embarrassed scent, and he figured if Knossis's skin hadn't been so dark, he would have been blushing.

Hank shrugged awkwardly, since he rested his head in his other hand. "Everyone likes sex a little differently," he said with a grin. "I'm a total bottom boy, so while I could fuck you, I wouldn't enjoy it very much."

Knossis grunted. "Huh." Then he looked over his shoulder. "That feels so damn weird."

Realizing Famine had pulled free of Knossis, Chissom teased over their shifter's soft chute muscle, massaging to soothe. "It does," he agreed. "That's why the one doing the fucking should always be careful when pulling out after the deed is done."

Sliding his cheek over Chissom's chest in a sort-of nod, Knossis groaned as he pushed back up onto his arms. "Sorry for crushing you," he muttered, then hissed as he pulled free. "Gods, it shouldn't have been possible for us to" — he grunted as he flopped on Chissom's other side while Famine chose to cuddle behind Hank — "get off so many times."

"That would be the need to bond at work," Famine told everyone, tracing his pale fingertips over Hank's hipbone, then over to Chissom's. "Once you all drank my blood, accepting a connection to me, your body craved my seed, my bite, and because I fed all of you, you needed each other as well."

Chissom nodded, thinking about that. "What about Hank?" he asked curiously, peering at their smallest lover, who lay cradled against his side with Famine curved around him. "We're sated, but shouldn't we still want Hank to fuck and claim us?"

Hank snickered as he grinned at him. "Um, how would I claim you?"

Famine threaded his fingers through Hank's hair affectionately. "While Hank will crave my blood every now and then, since he needs it to continue our bond, due to being human, he doesn't feel the need to claim us, too." Glancing between Chissom and Knossis, he explained, "Our paranormal natures recognize that on some instinctual level."

Chissom took that at face value. "So," he began slowly. "I guess we need to discuss the rest of it." As much as he hated interrupting the afterglow, Chissom knew they couldn't put it off much longer.

Knossis sighed deeply as Hank's brows furrowed.

Famine touched each of them in turn, the move soothing in a way that surprised Chissom. "How about we clean up first," the horseman offered. "Or we'll end up stuck together in cum and lube."

"I know we're just procrastinating, but yes, please," Hank immediately replied. Except, as he sat up, he winced and groaned. "Except, I'm not sure my legs will work."

To Chissom's surprise, Famine chuckled—actually *chuckled*. He also easily rose to his feet. Then he swept Hank into his arms and began heading toward the water.

Glancing over his shoulder, Famine called, "You both coming?"

Chissom exchanged a glance with Knossis, seeing the surprise in his eyes, too. Evidently, a well-sexed Famine was a much more relaxed one. After climbing to his feet, Chissom held his hand out to Knossis.

Once Knossis was on his feet, they both followed Famine into the water.

Five minutes later, clean but wet and cold, the foursome returned to the blanket.

Chissom pulled a couple of towels from the basket and handed one to Knossis, using his chin to indicate Hank. Their shifter turned and began drying off their human. Facing Famine, Chissom rubbed the towel over the horseman's body, enjoying the few quiet moments where he could explore without the pressure of sexual need.

"You know," Famine murmured, standing still under his ministrations. "I have the ability to dry us with a wave of my hand."

Chissom chuckled softly. "Of course you do." Offering his horseman a rakish grin, he quipped, "But where's the fun in that?"

Famine scoffed, his aristocratic features softening. "Of course."

Once everyone was dried, Famine did do the wave of hand thing . . . to clothe them. Chissom found them all in a similar pair of leather pants and tunic that their horseman favored. Just their colors were different. Famine dressed Chissom in shades of blue, Knossis in green, and Hank in yellow.

Hank looked down at himself, then shrugged. "Not my favorite, but it's okay."

"If you prefer a different color . . ." Famine lifted his hand, obviously ready to change what Hank was wearing.

Shaking his head, Hank settled on the blanket just in time for his stomach to growl. "Nope." He focused on Chissom. "A lot has happened. Feed me."

Chissom wasn't the only one who laughed even as he set out to obey.

CHAPTER ELEVEN

Hank took the container full of small sandwiches and placed three on the cloth napkin Chissom gave him. After taking a fourth, he passed the container to Knossis. As he popped the chicken and cheese sandwich into his mouth, he shifted his weight to the left, causing his ass to twinge.

Wincing, Hank made a mental note to take a soak in his room's jetted tub . . . with some bath salts.

"Are you well, Hank?" Famine touched his arm, concern filling his pale blue eyes. "Do you need healing?"

Thinking on that for an instant, Hank smiled and shook his head. He swallowed his bite of sandwich before telling him, "No, while I'm definitely feeling it, I like that sensation, too." Feeling his cheeks heat a little at the admission, Hank added, "I like the reminder that you all enjoyed my body so much."

Famine's smile turned predatory as a low growl rumbled from him. "I'm sure we'll all do it often, then." Then he reached out and threaded his fingers through Hank's hair.

To Hank's surprise, Famine pulled his face close and dipped his own head. He sealed his lips over Hank's, nipping his bottom one. On instinct, Hank opened, and Famine took advantage.

Hank found himself on the receiving end of a deep, probing exploration. The horseman teased his tongue and teeth. He gently suckled Hank's tongue, and in the end, when Famine released him, Hank was panting for breath, and his prick made a valiant effort to rise once more.

"Wow," Hank whispered, staring at Famine in surprise.

Smirking, Famine cocked his head and asked, "What?"

Swallowing hard, Hank admitted, "I didn't think you'd kiss."

Famine shook his head once, telling him, "Why would I limit myself when it's such an enjoyable activity?"

Hank grinned. "I'm glad I was wrong."

After a soft scoff and a wink, Famine released him. He turned his attention to the basket of fruit salad that Chissom had placed near the center of the blanket. Picking up a grape, Famine popped it into his mouth and chewed, humming in appreciation.

"Thank you for the meal," Knossis stated, bumping his shoulder into Chissom. He glanced around the area, frowning. "I can't believe we went on a fuck-spree with all the blood spray just fifty yards away." Then Knossis frowned. "Except, I can't see it or smell it." He focused on Famine. "Did you clean it up?"

As Famine swallowed the piece of watermelon he'd grabbed next, he shook his head. "No. War placed a glamour over it. We need to show it to Master Dante as proof of what happened." Famine smirked and added, "And we went on a fuck-spree, as you call it"—he waggled his brows suggestively—"because of our need to finish our bond." With a grin, Famine stated, "And I look forward to many more . . . fuck-sprees."

Chissom chuckled as Knossis snorted.

Hank appreciated the levity. Too bad it didn't last for more than a few minutes as they all chowed down on the food and wine Chissom had brought.

"I'm glad to see you all clothed."

The deep voice came from behind Hank, making him squeak. The fact that he recognized it didn't matter. He turned and glared over his shoulder, even though he didn't see War.

"Don't creep up on us like that, brother," Famine growled,

obviously not pleased, either. "I suppose our hour is up?"

"Afraid so." War appeared, no longer in his true form. His wings were hidden, as were his horns, and he appeared to be a massive black man. "Master Dante will be here any minute with Monte and the rest of the inner circle."

With a wave of War's hand, he removed whatever spell had hidden the scene of Glade's crime.

Hank cringed at the visual reminder of how close he'd come to death.

Chissom scooted over and wrapped his arm around him. With his other hand, he began packing up. Hank cuddled into his vampire's side and helped.

Knossis and Famine rose to their feet, and Hank realized how their roles were already beginning to form. He would always be protected, cared for. That knowledge warmed him and concerned him at the same time. Hank knew he wasn't a fighter by any means.

Am I a liability?

Evidently, Hank had broadcasted his thought.

Both Knossis and Famine turned, scowls on their faces. Chissom tightened his hold and cupped his jaw, tilting Hank's face to meet his gaze.

"Get that idea out of your head right now," Chissom ordered, frowning at him. "We need you." Releasing his chin, he waved at their lovers. "We wouldn't be able to make this work without you."

Hank glanced around at them all. Knossis nodded, a wry smile curving his full lips, while Famine just continued to appear stern.

"Why?" Hank didn't get it.

Famine eased his features into a soft smile. "I can already tell that Knossis and I are going to butt heads, while Chissom is going to rile my nerves." He narrowed his eyes as the vampire's grin turned cheeky. "You, my human" —Famine pulled Hank to his feet and into his arms—"are what you'd call the glue to this crazy relationship we've begun. You keep us—"

"From trying to kill each other," Knossis cut in bluntly. Resting his big hand on Hank's nape, he leaned close and pressed a gentle peck to his lips. "We're just learning about each other, but we all see it. You're our mediator. You soothe our more volatile natures, allowing us all to be together."

Relieved to be needed, Hank relaxed in Famine's hold. "Okay," he replied simply with a smile.

While Hank felt a little bad that he'd suddenly become so needy, he couldn't help his internal fears.

"You can be as needy as you like, my little human," Famine crooned into his ear before kissing his neck.

Hank tipped his head to the side, offering more room. "I'm going to have to work on this telepathic speaking thingy."

"We'll teach you," Chissom promised, rubbing his lower back.

War cleared his throat, reminding them of his presence.

Hank felt his cheeks heat as he burrowed into Famine's side. Except, when he peered at the other horseman, War's smile appeared . . . fond—happy even.

"It's good to see this side of you, Famine," War commented, his dark eyes holding warmth. "I think you made a fantastic decision."

"Well, so glad to have your approval," Famine replied dryly. Then his tone softened. "And I do believe you're right." Glancing around at his lovers, Famine added, "Although I'm sorry we met the way we did."

Knossis shrugged. "We never would have met otherwise." A look of relief took over his features. "And you helped me and my fox in a way you can't possibly imagine."

Famine gripped Knossis's nape and pulled him in for a slow, thorough kiss, practically squishing Hank between them, but he didn't mind. When they were done, Famine immediately grabbed Chissom and did the same to him, making

Hank chuckle.

"So, am I losing a vampire and donor?" Master Dante asked, announcing his arrival. "Or gaining another horseman?"

"Probably a little of both," Famine replied, releasing Hank. He stepped forward and held out his hand. "I'm the Horseman of Famine."

Master Dante took his hand and shook. "Thank you for saving my people."

Smirking, Famine glanced over his shoulder at them. "Ah, the pleasure is all mine."

After humming a little, Master Dante turned his attention to the mess that War had revealed. "Soooo," he rumbled, frowning. "What the hell happened, and how the hell did they get into our territory without being seen?"

"I'll check to see who was on patrol in the northern quadrants this morning," Monte stated from where he'd stopped to wrap his arm around War.

Nodding, Master Dante focused on Chissom. "Chiss? Report, please."

Chissom sighed deeply, then explained what had happened.

"Glade," Master Dante growled. "I didn't realize he'd stayed on with your skulk when Alpha Wilfred took over."

"I was surprised by his decision, too," Knossis admitted, rubbing the back of his neck. Scowling, he added, "Guess now I know why. He's out for revenge."

"We still need to know who the bears were," Chissom pointed out. "And how he contacted them."

Famine stated, "We know there's at least one witch involved."

Master Dante nodded. "That would explain how Glade slipped past our patrols." He peered at Kellan — the coven second. "Some kind of cloaking spell?"

Kellan looked thoughtful as he squinted at the blood and gore still covering the ground. "Maybe."

"Well, we won't get any answers until we talk to Glade." War rubbed his palms together, looking eager. "I say we go have a chat with him."

A shimmer appeared in the air right before Death appeared on his mount. "I agree with War." His eyes were narrowed, and he rested his scythe across his saddle's pommel. "Considering it affected my duties, I propose this falls under our jurisdiction."

"Because Glade attacked two of my people on coven ground, I plan to be there, too," Master Dante countered.

"Anyone got a phone?" Knossis asked. "I'll call my alpha and let him know a bunch of upset paranormals are on their way."

Master Dante tossed his phone to Knossis. "Maybe see if he can put Glade in custody."

"Yes, sir."

Then everyone waited as Knossis made the call.

CHAPTER TWELVE

Famine knew he was going to have to fight his instinct to keep all his companions as far away from danger as possible. The fact that Knossis was an enforcer for his skulk really didn't matter to him. He knew it should remind him that the big fox shifter could take care of himself, but it didn't.

After all, he'd stumbled upon them when they'd been near death. Their shredded and broken forms were still too fresh in his mind. While it had only been a few hours, he knew he couldn't lose any of them.

"Greetings, Master Dante," a deep voice sounded through the line. "How can I help you?"

"It's Knossis, Alpha Wilfred," Knossis corrected. "Master Dante loaned me his phone, since I came to coven lands in fox form."

"That's a bit of a long run, isn't it?" Alpha Wilfred questioned. "Why would you do that?"

Knossis cleared his throat, his scent of unease creeping into the air.

Famine reacted by resting his hand on Knossis's shoulder and massaging his nape while Chissom wrapped his arm around his waist. Even Hank must have picked up on the fact that something was bothering Knossis, for their human took the shifter's hand, twining their fingers.

After a quick smile at them all, Knossis admitted, "I left my car on a logging road to the west. It was only a few miles, and I needed to run as a fox a little before meeting up with Chissom." He met the vampire's gaze as he finished, "It was hard letting Chissom touch me knowing my mate was out there. It felt like . . . cheating."

"Even though, in your mind, you knew it wasn't." Alpha Wilfred sounded understanding.

"Right." Knossis leaned over and pecked a kiss to Chissom's lips.

Not anymore, though.

The words were broadcasted through their bond.

"So, why are you borrowing Master Dante's phone?" Alpha Wilfred asked. "What's going on?"

"Do you know the whereabouts of Glade Whistler?" Knossis didn't appear to be taking the direct approach.

"I know he invited me to a barbeque he's planning at his place with some friends this evening," was Alpha Wilfred's unexpected answer. "I found the invitation a little surprising actually, because he hasn't been around much after the council took away his father, Vivian, and her associates."

"That does sound fishy," Knossis replied, frowning. "Especially after he brought a bunch of bear shifters here to attack me, Chissom, and Hank."

"He did what?" Alpha Wilfred roared. "Are you okay? Are the others?" Snarling, he added, "Gods, I hope Master Dante knows I would never sanction an attack on anyone in his coven. I'll send Enforcer Dwyer to round him up right away. You're not in custody, are you?"

"I'm not in custody, and Master Dante knows you had nothing to do with it," Knossis told his alpha. After hesitating an instant, he stated, "Actually, I think you should hold off on sending Dwyer."

"That's good. Very good. Gods, the war Glade could have started between the coven and our skulk," Alpha Wilfred grumbled. "That moron. Wait." He must have registered Knossis's final comment. "Why?"

"If Glade is having a party, and he thinks your head enforcer is dead, then he might be making a play for being alpha," Knossis told him.

Seeing where Knossis's brain was going, Famine murmured, "Especially with the help he has."

Not surprisingly, Alpha Wilfred's sensitive shifter hearing allowed him to catch Famine's words. "Who's with you, Knossis?"

After placing the phone on speaker, Knossis listed everyone standing around before explaining, "The only reason Chissom, Hank, and I aren't dead is because Famine decided to bond with us." He smiled as he told his alpha, "He saved all our lives, and he also severed the pull I had to my mate. I feel . . . truly blessed this day."

"Famine," Alpha Wilfred murmured. "As in the Horseman of the Apocalypse Famine. That Famine?"

"Yes, Alpha."

"And you're bonded with him?" The alpha asked for clarification.

"Yes, Alpha," Knossis repeated.

"Okay," Alpha Wilfred responded, drawing out the word. "You've mentioned Chissom before, but who's Hank?"

Knossis lifted Hank's hand to his lips and kissed his palm before answering. "Hank is one of the coven donors." Then he frowned and corrected, "*Was. Was* one of the coven donors."

Hank smiled up at him. "Was," he repeated, obviously catching on that Knossis needed that confirmation.

Alpha Wilfred's deep sigh came through the line. "So, you think Glade is going to use those bear shifters to overthrow me and the rest of the inner circle." If Famine didn't miss his guess, he figured the alpha was rubbing his nose or forehead, maybe in agitation or frustration. "I'll round up a bunch of trackers, and we'll take them out."

"There could be magick involved," Famine cut into the

conversation. "Somehow, Glade's entire group crept onto coven grounds. My brothers and I noticed a magick signature that we thought had been wiped out."

"This is Death." The horseman crowded close so he could speak into the phone. "Whatever magick they're using is impacting the Moirai. They paired Knossis with someone unsuitable and unavailable, and they did not warn me of three impending deaths, which means I could not assign a demon to collect their souls."

"If Glade is involved with people like that," Knossis warned. "There's no telling what they could do to you and the rest of our people."

Alpha Wilfred finally seemed to realize the gravity of the situation. Issuing a low growl, he asked, "Well, I can't just sit here and wait for him to take my skulk."

"I have an idea," War stated with a malicious chuckle. "We're going to beat him at his own game."

Before the alpha could ask, Famine cut in, "That's War, and he has a deliciously malevolent smile on his face." Smirking, he asked, "What's your plan, brother?"

"Am I too late?"

Famine turned at the familiar voice and grinned as Pestilence appeared through a portal. "Right on time," he told the final horseman.

War laughed. "All four brothers together again for a bit of fun." He rubbed his hands together. "Let's take out the trash." Then War outlined his plan.

Famine didn't know how he'd managed to convince Hank to stay behind, but he'd done it. He wished he could have convinced Chissom to stay with Hank at the coven ranch house, too, but he flat out refused. Chissom had insisted on facing his attackers.

After giving Hank a hug and kiss, they'd left him in his

room. Their human had been waiting on a couple of others who were going to help him pack. While none of them had truly discussed where they would end up living, they all knew that Hank wouldn't be staying in his donor suite any longer.

With the time for Glade's barbeque approaching, Famine sat in the back seat with Chissom, while Knossis sat in a captain's chair in the middle. He didn't know why he needed the contact, but he didn't fight the urge. Famine rested one hand on Chissom's thigh and the other on Knossis's shoulder. His companions seemed to be of the same mind, for they placed a hand on top of each of his own.

As arranged with Alpha Wilfred, when their convoy arrived, Master Dante found the alpha walking a path near the road with Beta Bristol and Enforcer Dwyer. Famine sat back and watched the vampire master take the lead, exiting from the first vehicle with Enforcer Monte and Second Kellan. Two other enforcers stood beside that vehicle while no one in their vehicle exited. Famine could sense the presence of his brothers nearby, hidden by a glamour.

"Alpha Wilfred," Master Dante called, his voice cold with a hint of anger. "Is there a reason you sent shifters onto my coven lands to murder your enforcer as well as a pair of my people?"

Alpha Wilfred crossed his arms over his chest and frowned at Master Dante. "I did no such thing," he countered, frowning. "What possible reason would I have to cause problems between our two peoples?"

As expected, Glade came out of the nearby house along with others.

Famine really didn't like the pleased gleam in Glade's eyes as he glanced around at the growing crowd. He really didn't like the increasing number of innocents gathering, either. When War had outlined the plan, he hadn't mentioned what could happen if a fight broke out with so many around.

"Relax," Knossis rumbled, squeezing his hand. "Our people know how to stay out of the way when necessary."

After giving his shifter a small smile, Famine returned his attention to the confrontation.

"Then explain this bloodshed," Master Dante demanded, holding up his phone.

While Famine had no idea what picture Master Dante actually showed him, Alpha Wilfred still clenched his jaw and frowned deeply. "This had nothing to do with me," he stated, giving the phone back. "What makes you think it does? Perhaps your people were just in the wrong place at the wrong time when someone went after Knossis." Alpha Wilfred's lips twisted as he added, "I'd like my enforcer's body returned to us immediately."

Famine noticed Glade's cruel smile even though he cleared it quickly enough.

Then Glade moved to the top step of his deck and called, "Do you hear that, everyone?" He pointed at Alpha Wilfred. "Wilfred as alpha is dangerous. He's not fit to lead us." Crossing his arms over his chest, Glade continued, "Less than six months at our head, and he's already cost us our best enforcer. It's time for new leadership. Strong leadership." He lifted his chin haughtily. "Name me as alpha, just as my father wished before those vampires interfered, and now they're causing trouble again. They all must be stopped."

To Famine's surprise, the murmuring of the people around actually made it seem as if the members of Knossis's skulk were listening.

CHAPTER THIRTEEN

Knossis couldn't believe some of the whispered comments he could hear. While the black-tinted windows hid him from the eyes of his skulk-members, he could still hear them. Too many were expressing doubts about Alpha Wilfred's leadership.

Jackasses.

Then Knossis realized that most of the people congregating were friends with Glade. Of course, they would support him. Deciding it was time to put an end to Glade's bid to become alpha, Knossis opened the door and stepped out. Silence fell as he straightened to his full height. To his pleasure, he saw Glade's eyes widen.

"Rumors of my demise are a bit exaggerated," Knossis called, sweeping his gaze over the area. "I demand restitution from Glade Whistler for attacking my lovers, Chissom Minscote and Hank Everly."

Knossis noticed a few people glance at Glade before slinking away.

So long, fair-weather friends.

Then Knossis heard Famine's words of warning in his mind. *That means the rest of these foxes could very well be willing to fight at Glade's side.*

While Knossis hadn't needed the reminder, he appreciated Famine looking out for him. *We won't let that happen.*

Glade's eyes narrowed as he clenched his hands into fists. A muscle ticked in his jaw.

"You heard him, Glade," Alpha Wilfred stated, loud and

clear. "How do you respond?"

Scoffing, Glade shook his head. "I don't know what he's talking about." He sneered as he added, "*I* didn't attack his lovers."

"No, but you ordered it." Knossis rested his hands on his hips. "Who were those black bear shifters, and how did you contact them?" Lifting his chin, he stared down his nose at Glade. "How much did it cost you to try to assassinate your skulk's head enforcer and attempt to start a war between our people and the vampires?" Knossis shook his head. "What could you possibly think to gain by doing that? There would be bloodshed on both sides."

To Knossis's surprise, Glade's features smoothed into a conceited smirk. He leaned against the railing negligently as he crossed his arms over his chest. His shoulder lifted in a half-shrug as he focused on Alpha Wilfred, instead.

"I'll give you one more chance, Wilfred." The way Glade dropped their alpha's title set Knossis's teeth on edge. "Step down or die." Then Glade had the audacity to say, "Sorry, Dante. You're dead either way."

Knossis realized he'd grossly under-estimated Glade's delusional stupidity. Except, then over a half-dozen black bears lumbered from around the corner of the house. Glade's almost two dozen friends stripped their shirts, obviously preparing to fight.

Well, damn. Famine sounded amused. *Guess that's my cue.*

Famine exited the vehicle to stand beside Knossis with Chissom on his other side. "Your antics will fail, Glade," Famine drolled. "Do you really think you stand a chance against a horseman?"

Glade's cockiness slipped, but only for a second. He seemed to spot how his friends were looking his way for direction. The shifter lifted his chin, curving his lips into a sneer.

"You have no place here, Horseman," Glade declared.

"There's just one of you. Be on your way, and we won't take you out, too."

Famine tipped his head back and laughed, the sound full of cruelty. "Oh, silly little fox." Lifting a hand, he pulled a sheath of wheat from under the cloak he'd donned at the ranch. "Don't you know that there are four horsemen?"

Famine's brothers appeared, one on each side of the group of would-be attackers. Each carried their weapon of choice—War, a massive battle axe—Death, a scythe—and Pestilence, a hunter's bow—and sat upon their horses. In that same instant, Famine went from standing to sitting astride his own cream-colored horse.

Glade tried to back up a step and almost tumbled to his ass when his foot hit the step. Grabbing the railing for balance, he called, "What the hell are you even doing here?" His calm had well and truly shattered. "Shifter and vampire matters are of no concern of yours."

"You attacked someone in my vampire's coven," War commented, swinging his axe idly, the move making a *whoosh, whoosh* sound in the air. "Someone my vampire really, really likes. Hank is loved by everyone. How can you possibly think I wouldn't retaliate against you for making my vampire sad?"

Ouch. Thanks, War.

Knossis almost chuckled upon hearing Chissom's dry comment in his mind.

Relax. Famine did smirk. *He's just making idle conversation while we access just how dedicated Glade's friends are.*

"Hank wasn't supposed to be there," Glade claimed, shaking his head. Then he scowled and scoffed. "Besides, he's just a human. Plenty more where those came from to a vampire."

Unable to help himself, Knossis spoke up. "You're kind of an asshole, Glade." When the shifter in question snapped his attention to Knossis and glared at him, Knossis swept his gaze over the assembled group. "So, how expendable are each and every one of you?"

Knossis crossed his arms over his chest and waited. He noticed how while Glade's friends were now exchanging discreet glances, the bears did nothing but stand there. In fact, while Knossis had thought their cold dead eyes were a result of being assassins for higher, he wondered if that was actually true.

What the hell? Through their mental bond, Knossis reached out to Famine. *Do you think a circle of witches could control a shifter?*

Perhaps? Famine responded instantly. *What are you thinking?*

As Glade declared, "None of my friends are expendable," then swept his gaze to indicate the bears, "That's why we have these guys," the beasts still didn't respond.

Could those bears be under a spell? Knossis felt certain there was definitely something wrong with them. Out loud, he demanded, "Which of you is the leader of this bear den?"

When none of them even twitched an ear at Knossis's query, Famine hummed. *Yeah, I'm definitely scenting magick.*

Glade laughed. "They won't answer you. They can't." His gaze swept over the bears with the fond sympathy one would expect from an owner looking at a favored dog. "I bought and paid for them, so they only respond to my commands."

"What the hell have you done, Glade," Alpha Wilfred cut in, looking totally appalled. "What happened to these shifters?" He appeared completely scandalized. "Who did this to them?"

Smirking, Glade answered, "Wouldn't you like to know."

"In point of fact, I would." Death crept forward, his slender forefinger tapping the shaft of his scythe. His smile turned creepy as he stared at Glade, and Knossis was damn happy that look wasn't directed at him. "I have a feeling that tampering with a shifter's free will isn't the only thing they've been tampering with."

The color drained from Glade's face. "I-I can't tell you." He finally successfully backed up a step, putting him at the top of his porch. "They'll kill me."

Death let out a raspy chuckle. "And you think I'll do . . . what . . . to you?"

"Not me," Pestilence cut in, pulling an arrow from his quiver and knocking it to his hunter's bow. With a bland smile, he stated, "This arrowhead is tipped with syphilis." He grinned. "Don't worry. Even though you're a shifter, it'll still work." Pestilence drew back on the arrow. "Three . . . two —"

"Attack!" Glade shouted while lunging to the right.

Even as Knossis shifted, ready to shred any shifter that came near either of his lovers, he noticed Pestilence chuckle while putting away his arrow.

What the hell is his game?

Famine replied as he touched a fox shifter with his sheaf of wheat. *We needed a reason to attack. The Fates are picky.*

Knossis almost threw up when he saw the shifter shrivel in on himself, turning into little more than a mummified husk.

Then a bear lunged at Chissom, and Knossis attacked.

CHAPTER FOURTEEN

Extending his claws, Chissom spun to the left. He whipped out his arm, slashing the bear's hide as he lumbered past. As the bear turned back to face him, a wash of sadness flooded Chissom.

Now that Chissom was facing a bear one on one, he saw what had caught Knossis's attention. There was definitely something wrong with the shifter. His movements were jerky, and his attacks were awkward and uncoordinated.

Last time, Chissom had been completely overwhelmed by bears, which had taken him out. This time, he had plenty of help to disperse the shifters. When the bear lunged at him again, Chissom ducked, twirled, and slashed, slicing the bear's throat.

Chissom watched the shifter crash to the ground. It didn't rise as a massive amount of blood pooled beneath its head. Grimacing, Chissom hoped it would heal. He knew his people would do what they could to fix what had been done to the poor shifter.

Before Chissom could feel too bad about what he'd been forced to do, two fox shifters attacked. He glanced to his left, verifying that his lovers were well, before focusing on the pair. As Chissom spun away from the first one's lunge, he ducked under the second one's attack.

In truth, Chissom figured his lovers were probably doing better than himself. Knossis's fox was huge, his size almost rivaling that of a wolf. His mobility allowed him to easily outpace the movements of the uncoordinated bears. As far as

Famine went, everyone was trying to avoid the horseman. One touch of his wheat sheath would be the end of them.

When Famine had tucked the innocuous item into his cloak, he'd warned them all never to touch it. To anyone other than Famine, it would leech the life from them, leaving them nothing more than a dried-up husk.

After seeing it in action, Chissom would never second-guess Famine again.

Chissom pivoted while stabbing his claws into a lunging fox. With his vision hazed, allowing him to track the flow of blood through a person's body, he knew precisely where it was safe to hit. After all, Chissom wanted to incapacitate the morons, not kill them.

Yep, anyone who follows Glade is totally a moron.

Upon hearing Knossis's quip inside his head, Chissom couldn't help but smile. He quickly incapacitated another fox before a bear lumbered into the mix. Dropping to one knee, he rolled out of the barreling shifter's way . . . right into the path of a fox shifter's charge.

Chissom grabbed the medium-sized animal's upper front legs. Even as the animal's front claws raked over his arms, he shoved in the direction the beast had been leaping. Using the shifter's momentum, Chissom sent him flying over and past him . . . and right into the side of one of the SUVs.

The fox yipped and lay still.

Rolling back to his feet, Chissom ignored the dripping blood as he faced off against his next attacker — another fox duo. He noticed the cuts healed almost instantly, just as Famine had told them.

Good grief. Where do they keep coming from?

"That's enough!"

Chissom heard Alpha Wilfred's roar, and while the order didn't affect him the way it would one of the male's foxes, he still backed off. If the shifters were standing down, he wouldn't hurt them. They were blindly following a moron, after all.

Sweeping his gaze over the yard, Chissom spotted downed bears, injured foxes . . . as well as cowering ones. Knossis's massive deep-reddish-brown fox flanked a slightly smaller, orangish-red one—the alpha. Another fox of similar size to the alpha—probably the beta—flanked the alpha on his other side.

The trio stalked through the area, snarling and demanding submission from every still conscious shifter—all foxes.

As Chissom took in the group, he realized he didn't see a certain someone. "Where's Glade?"

"Right here."

Pestilence trotted around the corner of a house on his horse. The horseman held a fox by the scruff in his grip. The animal snarled and yipped, twisting and turning in the horseman's grip. Still, Pestilence easily kept the beast's claws and jaws from doing himself or his mount any harm.

Stopping before Alpha Wilfred, Pestilence shook Glade as if he were a recalcitrant pup. "I think this problem child should come with us," he stated, daring the alpha to counter him. "We have questions that he can answer that go well beyond just shifter matters."

Alpha Wilfred shifted swiftly and rose to his feet, unmindful of his nudity. With narrowed eyes, he stated, "After you get your answers, please give me the basics so I may report to the Shifter Council." He shook his head as he eyed Glade with distaste. "If he's been consorting with those who manipulate our kind in this way"—the alpha's focus slid to one of the down-but-still-breathing bears—"then the council needs to know what it could be up against."

"Of course." Pestilence dipped his head in agreement. When he began to turn his horse, the fox yelped piteously. Laughing, the horseman shook his head. "You should have thought of that before getting involved in matters beyond your control."

To Chissom's surprise, the fox in Pestilence's grip began to shift. The horseman swung from his saddle. He landed on his feet as he slammed the shifting beast to the ground. Pestilence kept his hand around Glade's neck as he resumed his human form, sprawled in the dirt.

Chissom spotted the hate-filled grin on his face.

"It's too late." Glade snickered as he swept his gaze around the group. He didn't seem to care at all that he was being held down by a horseman, and Chissom wondered if he had more than a few screws loose. Focusing on Master Dante, Glade taunted, "You may have saved Wilfred and your life, but you've forfeited your coven."

Then Glade began to laugh hysterically.

"What the hell does that mean?" Master Dante asked coldly, swiftly closing the distance between them.

Glade just continued to laugh spitefully.

Spotting the tell-tale sign of a shift in Knossis, Chissom rushed forward while grabbing the base of his shirt. He felt a hand on his shoulder and found Famine by his side. To his relief, as soon as Knossis began to rise to his feet, their horseman waved a hand and clothed their shifter.

That garnered a bark of laughter from War and a smirk from Death. Pestilence gave his brother a knowing look before refocusing on a still-cackling Glade.

"You'll answer our questions or end up in a world of hurt," Knossis declared. "What the hell was that supposed to mean?"

Glade just continued to grin.

Famine smiled coolly. "Allow me." He turned his head and eyed the dark trees to the left. "Beltine?"

From the darkness appeared a pale, muscular, white-winged demon—Beltine. The demon dipped his head at Famine. "Master."

Resting his hand on Beltine's blond head, Famine rumbled, "Thank you for coming. I have a request."

Beltine straightened, his chin lifting in stubbornness. "Anything for you, Master Famine."

Indicating Glade, Famine revealed, "This human has wards on his mind meant to keep out the probe of a horseman or a demon."

Chissom wasn't the only one who gasped.

In his mind, Chissom heard Famine share. *We all tried to penetrate Glade's mind while he was going on about how he should be alpha. Someone is protecting him.*

Ah. Chissom understood immediately. *Someone who doesn't want their involvement to be revealed.*

Exactly. Then Famine continued out loud, "Join me in pressing his shields. I believe that, together, we can destroy the ward and access what we need."

As one, Beltine and Famine crouched beside Glade. When they each placed a hand to either side of his head and began to murmur . . . something, the shifter finally stopped laughing. Instead, he started thrashing, desperately trying to break Pestilence's hold.

It didn't work.

Opening his mouth, Glade let out an unholy scream. Chissom grabbed Knossis's hand, needing the contact. Famine and Beltine didn't react, just continuing to grip Glade's head and chant in a language Chissom didn't understand.

Just as Chissom felt tempted to clamp his hands over his ears, Glade's eyes rolled to the back of his head, and he collapsed on the ground.

Famine and Beltine continued to touch Glade for another few seconds.

Then Famine yanked his hand away as if scalded. His gaze snapped to Chissom and Knossis. *Hank?* Famine called through their connection. When their human didn't answer immediately, he called for him again. *Hank, answer me!*

Still nothing.

"Famine, what is it?" Chissom couldn't wait any longer. He needed to know. "What's going on?"

After giving Chissom a tortured look, Famine turned and peered right . . . at Master Dante. "The witches who warded Glade's mind, who enslaved the bear shifters, and who are fucking with the Moirai's gifts . . . they're attacking your coven."

Master Dante's brows shot up. Then he yanked out his cell as he sprinted to the SUV.

With a tug, Chissom began to do the same.

Famine grabbed them both, stopping them. At his questioning look, their horseman told them, "This way is faster."

CHAPTER FIFTEEN

Hank rifled through his drawers, wondering what all he should bring. Thinking of Monte's relationship with War, he figured they could end up with more than one home. They would certainly have one in Famine's demon realm. The horseman had responsibilities, after all.

Would they end up with a home in Knossis's skulk as well as a small house on the coven ranch?

After Monte had bonded with War and Xerxes, Master Dante had built them a custom cabin a little ways away from the main ranch house. Would he do that for Chissom and Hank? They were only a wrangler and a donor, but Famine was a horseman, so surely they would need extra space. Plus, there was Knossis's fox to consider. He would need room to stretch his legs, sort of like Xerxes had a designated paddock to burrow in to his heart's content.

That meant Hank might have to end up having three piles. He decided not to get ahead of himself. Two piles first, then he could adjust later, if need be.

As Hank sorted his comfy lounging clothes into a demon realm stack and a human realm stack, he heard a knock on his door. "Come in," he called, moving to the door that led from his bedroom to his front living space. Upon spotting Stanton, Hank grinned widely. "Hey, Stan. What's up?"

The huge human had mated with their coven's vampire chef, Francois. While he looked like a big-ol' bruiser, he was actually a friendly teddy bear. He was kind and thoughtful with a heart of gold, even if some considered him a little slow.

Stanton just had an artist's brain that worked a little bit differently. Nothing wrong with that.

"Hey, Hank," Stanton greeted, a wide grin on his face as he entered. "I heard you snagged the final horseman." Then his expression faded to one of worry. "You're okay, right? You're not still hurt, right? Chissom's okay, too?"

Hank figured the tale of his and Chissom's escapade had run rampant through the coven, especially when they'd shown up with Famine.

Smiling, Hank nodded. "I'm good. We're both good." Patting Stanton on his lower arm, he added, "What are you up to?"

Stanton grinned broadly. "I brought snacks while we help you sort and pack."

Hank cocked his head. "Snacks?" His stomach rumbled at that idea. He could always eat, which explained the spare tire around his belly. Still, everyone at the coven accepted him as he was, never mentioning the fact that he really was a bit overweight. "We?"

His dark eyes lighting up, Stanton nodded. "Yeah. Jerome and Tony and Raphael will be here in just a sec." Then he hustled out of the room, calling, "I'll get the tray."

Smiling indulgently, Hank waited.

A second later, Stanton reappeared, pushing a trolley before him. There were three tiers on the metal carriage, each laden with trays. Several bottles of wine lay in the wine rack at the bottom, and Hank licked his lips, looking forward to whatever treats Stanton had brought.

After all, Stanton was bonded with the coven chef, and their chef was damn fantastic. It didn't matter what ended up under the dome covers—it would be sure to satisfy Hank's never picky taste buds.

Stanton had just begun removing lids, revealing a meat and cheese platter, a boat of cheese-stuffed mushrooms, and a big container of hot wings, when others began filing into the room.

Hank greeted Jerome — Stanton's best friend — and Tony — Jerome's younger brother and a new arrival at the ranch. Tony had recently bonded with Second Kellan, and he was still finding his footing in the paranormal world. Behind them was Raphael. The younger human had been with them for a year or so now, and he loved his life as a vampire's beloved and his work as a secretary, of sorts, for Master Dante.

"Hey, everyone," Hank greeted with a grin. "Thanks so much for the company."

As much as Hank hated to admit it, he already missed his men, and they'd only been gone an hour. When he'd agreed to stay behind, he hadn't anticipated how difficult the distance would be. Still, Hank knew he'd made the right decision, since all he would be was a distraction in a fight.

Instead, when his men returned, Hank would greet them with open arms, soothe any pains with kisses, and pamper the hell out of them with food, drink, baths, and massages.

Winners' sex will be fun, too.

Hank snickered at his thoughts, just assuming that his guys would always come out on top.

"Aww, you're thinkin' about your guys," Stanton teased, bumping him with his hip. "That's a great look. Huh, guys?"

Jerome chuckled softly, a wide smile curving his full, dark lips. "It sure is." Patting him on the back, he added, "Although, I have no idea how you could possibly keep up with three paranormals."

With wide eyes, Tony nodded. "Yeah." He sounded a little awed as he eyed Hank. "I still occasionally feel overwhelmed by the one I have."

Hank felt his cheeks heat, but he did his best to ignore it. Instead, he grabbed a tortilla chip and dipped it into the spicy chili cheese dip. "I've had over a decade to become accustomed to the appetites of paranormals," he explained to Tony before popping the bite into his mouth. Hank hummed appreciatively as he chewed and swallowed. Grinning at Stanton, he grabbed another chip. "Yum."

"I saved some boxes from our last supply delivery," Raphael claimed, grabbing a chip for himself. "With all the matings and changes going on, I figured they would come in handy eventually." With a bit of food still in his mouth, he mumbled, "They're in the barn tack room. Will you help me get them, Stanton?"

"Sure," Stanton immediately replied. He was always happy to help. "Let me open this wine for Hank first." As he spoke, he grabbed one of the bottles from the rack at the bottom. "Francois said it's his favorite."

Hank had just popped the cork when Hank thought he heard Famine's voice in his head.

Hank?

Swallowing the bite of stuffed mushroom he'd been chewing, Hank paused and cocked his head. *Famine?* He waited, but he didn't hear a reply. Hank didn't know how far their connection traveled or if it was based on distance.

"You okay, Hank?" Jerome tapped Hank's upper arm with the back of his hand. "You look a bit lost in thought. Wanna talk about it?"

Hank turned his attention back to the guys sitting and chatting in his room. Tapping the side of his head, he admitted, "Thought I heard Famine, but it could just have been my imagination." He shrugged and told him, "The bond is all so new, I'm still not certain about its limitations. Ya know?"

"I think Xerxes is here since Monte is with Dante and War," Jerome told him. "Want me to get him while the others get boxes? I bet he could answer a lot of your questions about being bonded with a horseman."

Pausing, Hank considered that for a few seconds. The prairie dog shifter had always been sweet and friendly. He tempered War's more lethal edges and Monte's more hotheaded ones.

"Yeah, if he's not doing anything." Hank grinned. "That would be great." Before Jerome could go anywhere, he added, "I'll try the intercom to call their suite first. Maybe he's there."

Jerome gave him a thumbs up before taking a glass of wine from Stanton. "Thanks, man."

Hank picked up the receiver on the wall, then punched a code that rang Enforcer Monte's suite. When it didn't ring, he frowned, hung up, and tried again. Hank started to do it a third time when he realized he didn't hear any tones whatsoever.

"Huh. That's weird," Hank muttered, pushing buttons. Nothing worked—not the direct call to the kitchens, the panic button, or the emergency line to the master's office. "Hey, guys." Worry flooded Hank. "Don't leave yet."

Nothing like this has ever happened before.

"What's up?" Raphael asked, snagging a crostini and sliding it through the artichoke dip. His brows furrowed. "Hank? What's wrong?"

Slowly placing the phone back onto the receiver, Hank murmured, "The intercom is out."

For a couple of heartbeats, no one said anything.

Finally, Stanton rumbled, "That's bad. Right?"

Hank nodded. "Um, yeah. I think it is." Once again, he tried to contact Famine, but he still didn't get a response. "Okay, I think we need to stick together," he decided, glancing between the guys. "And I think we need to talk to Xerxes. War is supposed to be with Master Dante, and he should know what—"

The lights went out, plunging them into darkness.

"Oh, fuck," Jerome muttered.

"Yeah," Raphael whispered.

Hank couldn't be certain, but he thought it was Tony who whimpered.

"Um, Jer?" Stanton asked uncertainly.

To Hank's surprise, his eyesight remained far better than he thought it would, even though there was only a sliver of moonlight coming through the windows. He saw Jerome reach over and take Stanton's big hand in his own. The huge human immediately seemed to relax.

"Okay, everyone," Hank whispered, thinking quickly. "It's time to arm ourselves."

In a small voice, Raphael whispered, "With what?"

Good question. Good question indeed.

Peering around his room, Hank weighed his options.

CHAPTER SIXTEEN

Famine zipped himself and his companions along a lei line. As soon as he was within a half-mile of the ranch house, he felt it — magick. Uncertain what he was walking into, he found an alternate exit a little ways away for them to rematerialize.

"Holy shit," Knossis muttered, staggering a little. "What the hell was that?" Just as quickly, he looked around. "Where are we?"

"About a mile east of the ranch house," Chissom answered, having obviously recognized the area. He focused on Famine. "Is that the way you travel?"

"When in the human realm, yes," Famine answered honestly. "There's witch activity near your ranch house. I didn't want to materialize in the middle of it."

"Understandable." Chissom turned and began jogging toward the ranch. "Tell me when you feel something," he ordered as Famine and Knossis hurried to flank him. Then he pulled out his cell phone. After a second, Chissom cursed. "Fuck, the ranch phones are out."

When Famine still didn't get a response from Hank through their telepathic connection, his gut tightened. "I never should have left him behind," he muttered, shaking his head. "The safest damn place would have been at my side."

"Hindsight is always twenty-twenty, Famine," Knossis stated, a scowl etched into the big man's features. "We'll find Hank, and he'll be just fine."

Famine jerked a nod, then skidded to a stop. His companions nearly rammed into him, and he put out his arms to stop them before they hit the barrier. If they had, not only would his lovers have been hit with an electric jolt, but it would have alerted any number of witches as to their location.

"There's a shield here," Famine explained upon spotting their questioning looks. "I need to form a hole, or we'll have trouble."

"We'll take care of it, Master."

Famine turned, surprised to see not only Beltine there, but also two dozen of his oldest demons. "Thank you," he stated gratefully. So many times, he forgot that he had help. As Famine eyed his minions, he warned, "These witches are powerful, so be careful. I don't want to lose any of you."

Beltine grinned, showing off a mouthful of pointy white teeth. "Thanks, Master, but you won't." With a jaunty wink, he turned toward the shield and added, "In less than a year, I get my amina. Not gonna jeopardize that."

Chuckling softly, Famine watched and waited as four of his demons joined Beltine. They lifted their hands, palms out, and whispered in the harsh, guttural demon language. In seconds, the shield glowed a sickly red color.

"Oh, damn," Knossis mumbled. "That doesn't look natural."

"No, it's not," Famine confirmed. "That shade denotes blood magick. These witches are into human sacrifice." Remembering the loss of not only his demons but his brothers' over the last few months, Famine amended, "Or demon sacrifice." Shaking his head, he mused, "Sacrificing demons would explain their power and why their spells are affecting the Moirai. The magick is twisted, warping everything it touches."

Knossis cracked his knuckles. "Then it's time we take them out."

"Your shifter is right," War stated, announcing his presence, a growl in his voice. "Xerxes is in there, and Monte and

I can't reach him."

"Same with Hank," Famine admitted.

"We'll have a hole in five ... four ... three ... Dasgar, more power," Beltine instructed. "Perfect." Then he focused on a different demon. "Lerios, keep it there. Hold it steady."

Famine could feel the demons combining their power, with Beltine monitoring and tempering their efforts with his own abilities. He realized his demon would make a fantastic general and prayed to the gods that he would get through this safely so he would have that chance. In the next instant, a small arched opening appeared in the shield, and Famine could think of little but getting to Hank.

"You two go ahead," Death urged to him and War. "Pestilence and I will search out the witches and take them out."

Even though Famine knew Death didn't need the reminder, he couldn't help but say, "We need a few alive."

Pestilence snickered as he knocked an arrow. "This little baby will give the recipient the worst stomach bug in history. She'll find the nearest tree and not be able to move for hours."

Famine grimaced as Chissom muttered, "That was more than what I needed to know."

War and Monte ducked through the hole in the shield, and Famine immediately followed. He sensed his companions at his back, but he suddenly couldn't feel their presence in his mind. Growling under his breath, he vowed to destroy whatever circle of witches was dabbling in such dark magick.

Glancing behind him, Famine spotted Pestilence and Death moving through the hole and disappearing in opposite directions. He exchanged a tight smile with Knossis and Chissom, then focused ahead. Famine had his own task to complete — find and secure Hank, then save the coven.

When War and Monte eased to a stop, Famine came up behind him. He saw his brother point at a trio of witches standing on the front step of the ranch house. They were openly casting spells at it, but the door was holding.

"Bespelled it after bonding with Monte," War whispered in explanation.

"That's a lot of open ground," Famine commented, eyeing the thousand yards of open paddock.

"Not for a vampire," Chissom countered.

Monte nodded once. "Especially if we have a distraction." He looked pointedly at War.

Growling under his breath, War grumbled, "Son of a bitch. Fine."

Famine wasn't following. "What's the plan?"

"Shield Knossis so he doesn't get hit with a spell," War ordered, pointing at the fox shifter. "Then the three of us walk right toward the witches, exchanging strikes." With a smirk, he pointed at their vampires. "Those two will sprint in around the side of the house and slice open their necks."

"No trying to incapacitate them?" Famine couldn't help but tease.

War grinned evilly. "We'll leave that to our brothers."

"Perfect." Famine grabbed Chissom and pressed a hard kiss to his vampire's lips. "Don't get hurt."

Chissom grinned. "Same to you."

Famine released Chissom, and his vampire sprinted into the shadows. Turning to Knossis, he kissed him lightly before ordering, "Unfortunately, a fox against three witches isn't much help. I'm sorry, my shifter."

Knossis nodded once. "I get I'm out of my element here. I'll stay behind you and safe."

Relief filled Famine that Knossis understood. "Thank you." Then he lifted a hand and weaved a glamour spell around him, making him invisible to all but a horseman . . . or his bonded mates.

In the next instant, shoulder to shoulder with War, Famine marched toward the witches. "You're in our way," War called. "Leave now, and I may consider letting you go." He cracked his knuckles before hefting his battle axe. "Of course, I probably won't."

"Subtle," Famine murmured.

War shrugged. "I don't do subtle."

Chuckling, Famine watched as the three women exchanged looks, then turned to face them. "No, you don't." Narrowing his eyes, he added, "Neither do I." Raising his voice as he sped up his strides, "In Master Dante Mannis's name, your attack is considered a paranormal act of war, and your lives are forfeit."

The witch on the right flung a red bolt at Famine. With a quick word, he absorbed it with a shield. He saw the way it crackled around the edges, surprised — and annoyed — by the power behind it.

Many demons died to give them that power. Time to take it back.

After exchanging a look with War, Famine and his brother went on the offensive. They aimed shots of electricity at the women, scorching the wood of the porch when they missed their shields. It didn't take long for them to force the trio to the left, away from the front door . . . and their vampires took the opening.

Monte and Chissom sprinted around the corner and, with a few swipes of their claws, tore out the three women's throats, their blood spraying over the side of the house, the boards of the deck, and the pillars that held it.

Before the dead women had even hit the planking, Famine yanked Chissom into his arms. He pressed a hard kiss to his lips for a second before drawing away. Even as he noticed War doing the same with Monte, he grabbed Knossis and kissed him, too.

Once Famine had tasted both his companions' tonsils, he released them. "Let's go get Hank."

Chissom replied, "Good idea," as Knossis nodded.

EPILOGUE

Knossis sat in the huge study with Hank curled up on his lap. Famine stood off to the side, talking to his brothers. Chissom approached, carrying a huge tray laden with plates and drinks.

"You feeling okay?" Chissom asked as he placed the tray on the coffee table before them.

Knowing his vampire directed the question at Hank, Knossis didn't bother to answer.

Smiling, Hank rolled his eyes. "Of course, I'm good. You all stopped those witches before they could even get into the house."

"That was still way too close," Master Dante stated, annoyance filling his tone. As Chissom gave a glass of wine to Hank and a beer to Knossis, Dante hollered, "Brothers, can I get a report, please?"

That drew the attention of each of the Four Horsemen of the Apocalypse.

Knossis bit his lip, wondering how the guys would respond to the vampire master's demanding tone. He watched Famine exchange looks with his brothers.

Then . . . War grinned broadly as he strode forward. "Sure, D. We got a report for you." He grabbed Xerxes from where he was sitting in a large chair. After plopping onto the cushion, settling Xerxes on his lap, War slung his arm around Monte's waist, tugging him close. "The circle is now officially defunct." His eyes held a malicious gleam as he added. "Dead. D-E-D. Dead."

Famine rolled his eyes, although he appeared amused at War's antics. "We found out that after Ferris was taken by the Shifter Council, Glade started putting out feelers for others who were unhappy with the new rules the council was enforcing." Heading toward them, he continued, "The witches noticed and contacted Glade. When he started talking about demons and horsemen, well" — Famine growled as he sat on the other end of the sofa with Chissom in the middle — "they were happy to offer him *anything* he wanted to get access to War and his minions."

War's countenance darkened as he growled, "They were going to kidnap Xerxes and use him against me."

Resting his hand over the back of the sofa, Famine teased his fingers over the shoulders and hair of each of them, seeming to need the contact. "They didn't even know about Hank, but if they had, he would have been a target, too."

Knossis reached up and squeezed Famine's forearm. "Hank is safe. He's here." He tightened his arm around their human where he relaxed curled up on his lap. "We saved him."

Famine tipped his head and inhaled Chissom's scent, seeing as he was the closest to the horseman. After a few seconds, he smiled at Knossis. "I know."

After clearing his throat, Master Dante asked, "And what of the bears?"

Groaning, Death admitted, "We can't do much for them. Wrong kind of magick."

Pestilence cut in, "So we'll take them to shifters who may be able to."

Death nodded. "There's a biker gang of shifters who have warlocks riding with them," he explained. "They've also dealt with witches before. We hope they can help."

"Then not a bad win," Dante mused. "Although, I wish it hadn't happened so close to home."

"Unfortunately," Famine stated, his fingers tightening on Knossis's shoulder for a few seconds. "We're still searching for what the witches called The Red Book. It contains the instructions they used to track demon movement, capture them, and use their blood in spell-casting." Grimacing, Famine admitted, "Only two witches knew the location of it, and both died in the attack. Now we'll have to retrace their movements to guess at a location."

Pestilence grimaced. "We need to destroy that book."

Master Dante sighed deeply as he took a glass of whiskey from Kellan. "One step forward, two steps back."

"Oh, I don't know," Chissom countered with a grin. "We stopped Glade from overthrowing his skulk. We stopped witches from fucking with the fates, the horsemen, and our coven. We freed shifters from enslavement . . . sort of." Lifting his hand, he ticked off the items. "We've roped another horseman to our coven." Chissom waggled his eyebrows at Famine, who just smirked. "And not only did we learn where the bad guys are getting their information, but we're coming together as paranormals."

Chissom hummed. "That's gotta be, like . . . eight steps forward and only one step back."

Master Dante barked a laugh as he nodded. Then he lifted his whiskey tumbler. "To eight steps."

After a round of "Eight steps," Knossis took a swig of his beer, and—for the first time in so very long—he looked forward to whatever his next step ended up being.

YOU MAY ALSO ENJOY THE FOLLOWING FROM EXTASY BOOKS INC:

Bobbing with A Giant Octopus
Charlie Richards

Excerpt

Dare, are you busy?"

Turning away from where he'd just finished stocking the security office's shelves with coffee, sugar, and other basics to face Alpha Kaiser, Dare Winterwall grinned at the fellow shifter and leader of their pod. "Was just thinking about scouting the park for a one-night stand," he told him, not at all abashed to admit he was thinking about getting laid. "But that can wait. What's up?"

Dare had lived for nearly a century in his giant octopus form, never feeling safe on land. When Kaiser had tracked him down and had shared his vision of building World of Aquatica—a marine park utilizing aquatic shifters—he'd been flattered to be offered an enforcer position. Even after being mostly human for over a decade, he was still making up for lost time.

"Graham and Eban have gone to fetch Graham's vampire friend, Price Litner," Kaiser told him, crossing his arms over his chest. His eyes narrowed, and his brows drew together.

Leaning a hip against the counter, Kaiser added, "I guess he's run into an issue, and he's running from the military."

"Ah, damn." Dare shook his head. "So is he coming here to hide, then? I know Eban feels a bit beholden to him considering Price saved Graham's life before they even met."

Kaiser nodded. "He is, although I think he's coming to see if he's going to be accepted by me." Easing his features into a smirk, he told him, "As long as he's truthful with me, I don't have an issue with him hiding out here for however long he needs."

"Truthful?" Dare asked curiously. "About what?"

"Why he's not part of a coven." With a shrug, Kaiser lowered his arms and pushed away from the counter. "When I first learned of Eban's feelings about how Price saved Graham, I asked Master Bercham to inquire about him from the council. He's been labeled rogue, and I want to know why."

Dare hummed as he began following Kaiser out of the security office. "Makes sense."

Master Aldor Bercham led a coven based south of Sacramento. They'd always had a good working relationship with the coven. Once or twice, they'd even utilized a vampire's ability to alter a human's mind when they'd seen or learned something they shouldn't.

"Has Price been living near Master Bercham's territory?" Dare asked curiously. He waved at Rawlins, a shifter manning their security office's front desk. "Sorry, Rawlins." Winking, Dare tipped his chin toward their alpha. "I don't think I'll make it to the bar tonight. Duty calls."

Rawlins sighed as he nodded. "Yeah, figured as much when I saw you come in, Alpha Kaiser."

Kaiser chuckled softly. "Maybe Gracin or Saul would accompany you," he offered, referring to a couple of other single shifters. "I bet they would enjoy a night out."

Grinning, Rawlins nodded. "Good idea, Alpha."

Stepping out of the office, Dare felt the warm spring air wrap around him. He loved that it had once again become warm enough to work in polo shirts. The soft short-sleeve fabric showcased his massive muscles, which always made it easy to attract a willing bed warmer for the night. With so many humans coming and going through the park, Dare never had any trouble finding someone interested in a little fun between the sheets.

When a blond-haired human gave him the once-over and a flirty smile, Dare winked back at him.

Too bad I can't stop to talk to him. Get his name and number.

"You're already thinking about fucking that human," Kaiser murmured, his voice soft enough for Dare's sensitive shifter hearing to pick up, but it wouldn't carry to the humans around them. "Why don't you get his number? We still have thirty minutes before I expect Eban to return."

While Dare appreciated his alpha's offer, he shook his head and picked up his pace. "Naw. I don't want to make a promise to some guy if this takes longer than you think." Seeing Kaiser arch one black brow, Dare realized how that sounded. "Uh, not that I'm second-guessing you."

Kaiser snorted and grinned. "Of course not."

Picking up their pace, they made their way to a golf cart parked around the corner from the office. Dare climbed onto the passenger seat, tucking his long legs a little awkwardly. At six-foot-six, he didn't fit in the vehicle really well, so he appreciated that he wasn't driving.

Dare enjoyed watching the scenery as they headed out of the park, driving along the windy paved trail that led to the complex of apartments and condos. Many of the employees working at the park were shifters, so Kaiser had designed homes for them just north of the park. An elevator to a massive underground grotto was housed in the largest building, and any of the shifters could utilize it. They also owned a couple of private beaches in that direction, too.

"Ah, looks like they arrived early," Kaiser commented as he pointed toward Eban's parked truck. "Must not have hit much traffic."

"Or Eban speeded," Dare tossed out his own idea.

Kaiser chuckled as he nodded and parked.

Following Kaiser into the building, Dare noticed an intriguing scent. He cocked his head and inhaled deeply. "Huh." His blood heated and flooded south. "Do you smell that?"

Glancing his way, Kaiser nodded. "Sure. I smell that a vampire has passed by here recently."

"No, not that." Dare shook his head. "I mean . . ." After inhaling again, he couldn't fight the arousal surging through him. "Oh!"

Realization hit.

"Oh, what?" Kaiser asked as he opened the door to a room he used as his office. Holding it open, he allowed Dare to pass. Evidently, Kaiser noticed the arousal in Dare's scent. "Something you want to share with the class?"

Dare came to a stop a few feet inside and stared at the stranger standing on the other side of the room. The vampire was wiry and toned and stood around six-foot-one. His nape-length, pale-blond hair had been slicked back from his face, accentuating his high-cheek-boned features.

"You're my mate," Dare declared, in awe of the gorgeous male that Fate had deemed his.

Upon hearing Dare's voice, Price snapped his focus to him, and his pale-blue eyes widened. His lips parted, but he didn't speak.

Eban slapped Price on the shoulder, and amusement filled his tone. "Congrats, Price. Seems you're no longer rogue. Welcome to the pod."

Dare grinned widely as he continued to admire his mate. "Hell, yeah. No more one-night stands."

ABOUT THE AUTHOR

Charlie started writing fantasy when she was eight, and after stumbling onto her first erotic romance at age nineteen, she realized her true calling. She now focuses on writing gay erotic romance, normally of the paranormal variety, with heroes of all kinds. With the help and support of her husband, Charlie finally fulfilled one of her life-long goals . . . move to acreage with her horses. You can often find her curled up with her laptop and a cup of tea or glass of wine, creating her next adventure. Charlie enjoys exploring the mountains of her new Oregon home on horseback, 4-wheeler, or motorcycle.

She can be reached at ch.richards2010@yahoo.com
Or visit her at www.charlie-richards.com

www.ingramcontent.com/pod-product-compliance
Lightning Source LLC
Chambersburg PA
CBHW070504130626
46555CB00003B/1159